The Death of a Confederate Colonel

The Death of a Confederate Colonel

Civil War Stories and a Novella

by Pat Carr

THE UNIVERSITY OF ARKANSAS PRESS
FAYETTEVILLE • 2007

11   10   09   08   07   5   4   3   2   1

Text design by Ellen Beeler

⊗ The paper used in this publication meets the minimum requirements of the
American National Standard for Permanence of Paper for Printed Library Materials
Z39.48-1984.

Library of Congress Cataloging-in-Publication Data

Carr, Pat M., 1932–
The death of a Confederate Colonel : Civil War stories and a novella / by Pat Carr.
    p. cm.
  ISBN-13: 978-1-55728-835-6 (pbk. : alk. paper)
  ISBN-10: 1-55728-835-6 (pbk. : alk. paper)
  1. United States—History—Civil War, 1861–1865—Fiction. 2. Historical fiction,
  American. 3. War stories, American. I. Title.
  PS3553.A7633D43 2007
  813'.54—dc22

                                                              2006037502

For Stephanie, Shelley, Sean, and Jennifer,
who gave me my fifteen minutes

Contents

Acknowledgments

The stories in this collection have been published in slightly altered versions in *Arkansas, Arkansas*; *Backbone: A Journal of Women's Literature*; *Caprice*; *Home and Beyond*; *Our Brothers' War*; *The Rio Grande Review*; *Southern Magazine*; *The Southern Review*; and *Writing on the Wind*. Thanks is extended to the Prairie Grove Battlefield Museum for use of the diary featured in "Diary of a Union Soldier."

A staged reading of *Leaving Gilead* was performed at the 2000 Judy and A. C. Greene Literary Festival.

Diary of a
Union Soldier

EAD BRANCHES WERE scraping so resolutely across the roof that it was only when the wind slackened that the thud of the cannons echoed up from the grove. But even as she heard the muted guns, she didn't associate them with an actual engagement, and when she saw him at the steps, not having heard him crash through the woods, just seeing him appear in silence at the porch, she didn't realize he'd come from a battle.

He put out a hand toward the post for support, and she could tell he was hurt, and perhaps that was why she wasn't afraid, why she opened the door as he staggered up the steps.

"I'd appreciate a drink of water, ma'am," he said with soft politeness. "I noticed your well, but it'll take considerably more strength than I've got just now to raise the bucket."

She couldn't see any blood on him, but she thought he might collapse along the porch boards any second. "You look like you could use a chair as well as some water," she said.

"Yes, ma'am."

She opened the door wider, and he lurched by her, angled across the room until he cracked into the bed rim and dropped face down on the coverlet.

The hand he had tucked in his pocket fell loose, and then she saw the blood, trickling down the back of his hand, separating at the knuckles, dripping off the fingers.

She stepped inside and closed out the wind. "You'll bleed to death unless you staunch that."

"Yes, ma'am," he said as politely, in a voice muffled by the bed quilt.

She walked over and looked down at him. He was a tall man, possibly Sy's age, muscular and fit, but the cheek turned toward her had begun to gray.

"And I guess you can't do that without help either."

"No, ma'am."

She stood a moment longer, but the puddle of blood beneath his hand was widening. She raised her voice before his closed eyes as if somehow his wound had deafened him as well. "You'll have to shift a bit for me to get your jacket off."

"Yes, ma'am."

He gingerly twisted his torso. "Ah-h-h." Droplets of sweat beaded his forehead.

"That's enough. I can twist the buttons through." She spoke in the same, too-loud tone to protect his feelings, to cover the cry she knew had been involuntary.

The brass belt buckle and the buttons were cold, but the dark wool itself was sweaty and warm to her touch. She hadn't seen a Yankee uniform before, and she was impressed at how sturdy and new the jacket was.

"I don't have anything against you Union soldiers." She kept talking in case he moaned again and would be shamed at her overhearing. She worked the buttons through the stiff buttonholes. "Sy voted to stay with the Union, but when the state decided to go Confederate, he joined up with the rest. Everyone around here pretty much went along. Is it your arm?"

"And I'd guess my back," he said through clenched teeth.

He opened his eyes directly before hers, and she saw they were the brilliant green of new hickory leaves. She wondered why she hadn't noticed them first thing.

"Crabb fell right beside me, and when I stooped to help him up, some Secesh got me from the brush," he said in a single breath, his jaw rigid.

She had the jacket unbuttoned and was starting to ease it off the gray undershirt.

"Crabb was dead," he said in the same clamped voice, as if his friend were someone she knew and had asked about. "Go ahead, ma'am. It's no use to keep stopping. Just pull the sleeve off all at once. Ah-h-h."

She realized she was clenching her own jaw as she tugged the sleeve away from the bloodied hand.

The gray undershirt had become so soaked that the cloth itself seemed to have dissolved into blood. A slaughtering smell filled the room, and she shallowed her breath against it. "You'll have to raise up and help me get off your shirt. I can't bandage you with it on."

He closed his eyes, gave what she took as a nod.

"M-m-m-m," came through his lips, so tightly shut they'd almost disappeared, but he balanced himself on the elbow still in the jacket sleeve and swayed upright.

She quickly pulled the jacket off his good arm and tossed its heavy bulk to the floor. She undid the two buttons of the undershirt and peeled it back from his head, then down away from the wound. It reminded her of the bloody skin of a frying rabbit as she flung it after the jacket.

Fresh blood instantly coursed down his arm. She forced herself to lean over and peer at his shoulder. Blood was welling up around the torn flesh and shredded muscle and running down his bare back.

She shivered and tried to control the shaking of her hands as she hurried to the chest at the foot of the bed. Sy always killed rabbits and chickens for her, and she averted her eyes from the blood already caking on her fingers. "The ball's probably still in your back." She tried to sound calm as she opened the trunk, but she could hear the quaver in the words. "As soon as you get back to your own side, a doctor can pick it out for you. I'm just going to stop the bleeding."

The extra sheet was fortunately on top, so she didn't have to bloody any of her other things looking for it. She lifted it out, closed the lid, and bit through one corner of her hemstitching. The muslin had been washed to the consistency of baby linen, and it tore in easy strips.

She stood up again to lay each frayed ribbon of cloth on the bed, continued biting, tearing until she'd ripped up the complete rectangle of the sheet. The rushed activity had replaced her inner shaking, and when she told him not to move, her voice was calm again.

He'd sagged aside as if unaware he wasn't sitting erect, and he didn't try to straighten as she held one end of the makeshift bandage at his collarbone and began to wind the cotton strips as tight as she could around his bleeding shoulder and back. She concentrated on the new white cloth that twined around and around, and tried to ignore the first patches of cotton that had soaked scarlet in a second. She bound the arm against his side, wrapped the widths of cotton, anchoring the end of each strip with another winding.

Then she was reaching for her final strip, twisting it over the others, holding it while she awkwardly plucked a pin from the cushion on the washstand. When the end was secure, she checked the thick layer of white bandaging and was certain only a doctor could have done any better. She took a deep breath.

But the man had his eyes closed, and she couldn't think how to congratulate her own doctoring. His skin was dark beside the white of her ruined sheet. And black hair grew on his chest, tangling in the hollow between the muscles. Sy's chest was as devoid of hair as Scofield's, the slave Sy hired from Doc Tibbens at harvest time, the two of them haying side by side, their bare chests glistening in the sun. The Yankee's chest hair was thick, as dark as that tumbling over his forehead, and she was suddenly embarrassed by his seminudity.

"You lie back while I get that water," she said quickly.

He leaned toward the foot of the bed, and she grabbed the pillow to change it for him. She barely got it plumped into position before he relaxed onto it with an audible sigh. He hadn't opened his eyes.

She scooped up the pitcher and went outside.

The sunlight spread thin through the leafless trees, but the wind had softened, warmed to more like spring than December, and she heard the distant cannons as she lowered the bucket. Sy had been good about bringing in water, too, and she was awkward with the rope even though he'd been gone half a year.

It took her longer than usual but at last she struggled the bucket onto the stone rim and tilted it to fill the pitcher and rinse her hands. The steady firing in the grove continued as she went back to the house.

The man was deep asleep, and she stood looking down at him.

He was what any woman would call good-looking, with all those black curls and long black eyelashes, those startling green eyes beneath the closed lids, and his lips seeming too soft to belong to a man. He was in all ways different from Sy.

But then she reminded herself that even a strong, fit man asleep with a bare chest in a December cabin could take cold, and she returned to the trunk for her company quilt. As she gently tucked it around him and straightened, she saw his jacket and undershirt wadded together, staining the floor.

She could just kick them outside, push them off the porch with her shoe, but even as she thought about doing it, she knew she wouldn't. She, of course, had to rinse them out and let them dry before the fire. Any woman would do the same.

She stacked an armload of juniper onto the already burning logs, filled the kettle, and hung it over the fire. She brought in the tub from the porch and lifted the undershirt and jacket one at a time with thumb and forefinger, but just as she tipped the jacket over the edge of the washtub, a small book fell from the pocket, flopped like a dead white bird on the floor.

She reached down for it, and in the fire glow she could see paragraphs of tiny script separated by dates. It was obviously a diary.

The cover was missing, but the spine had been sturdily sewn and the pages seemed intact.

She put it on the table and glanced at him.

The quilt covered him from chin to boot tops, but she could picture the hand that had grasped the newel post. It was a lean hand with long slender fingers well able to write those neat lines of script.

Steam from the tea kettle claimed her attention, and she lifted the handle with a swatch of her skirt, poured the boiling water over the jacket and shirt. Blue dye and blood instantly blackened the water.

She sloshed the clothes around with her broom handle, pressed them against the metal tub side, but she could see that to wash out the blood would take more water, a scrub board, and some strong lye soap, so after a few minutes she leaned the broom against the fireplace again, squeezed out the jacket and shirt, and draped them over a chair near the fire.

She emptied the dark water off the edge of the porch, not sure when she went back in if the blood stench had lessened or if she'd merely become used to it.

She brought in more wood and added more logs to the fire before she sat down at the table. There'd have to be a good blaze going all night since she'd be sitting up.

When she lit the candle, the flame immediately glittered on the spirals of ink in the diary as if the words had been freshly inscribed, and her eyes registered a date.

September 5th, 1862.

That day she'd have chopped wood, hauled water, foraged a basket of windfall apples to pare and dry. But there'd be no cause to keep a diary unless she intended to record more than that, unless she planned to write the truth in it. And yet what good would the truth do anyone? She was already a party to that truth, not needing to write it down to know it, and the words would only wound Sy if he chanced to read them.

She glanced again at the man on the bed.

The quilt raised and lowered slowly with his breathing.

But the Yankee's diary probably wasn't personal.

No man she'd ever met would have written a close personal thing in a book that anyone could happen upon. Men seemed to feel they had to guard themselves to disguise what they weren't for a woman's benefit.

6

And the Yankee was probably like that. Good-looking men were always careful to maintain the myths. He'd have taken precautions not to write anything that would give away more about himself than he wanted to his wife.

He was also certain to have a wife. Any man as well favored as he was would have one. Possibly he was even on a second wife like Sy. But, unlike Sy, he'd have married some younger woman who would adore him.

His little coverless book with its fine script wouldn't be revealing, and she'd never have another opportunity to learn about the war.

Yet even as she told herself the diary would be the only way she could glimpse that masculine world, she knew her rationale was no justification. She knew how she'd feel if someone read a diary she'd written.

She quietly pulled her chair up to the table, pushed the diary directly into the candlelight.

But then he'd never know if she read a page or two of his diary. And even if he knew, he'd likely not care.

The candlelight danced in the loops of his letters, and she stiffened her shoulders for another moment.

Why should she have qualms about reading the diary anyway? He *was* the enemy.

She looked down at the page.

September 5th, 1862.

We arrived at St. Louis at ten A.M. It was an exceedingly hot day, and many of us, unaccustomed to being bundled up in the amount of woolen goods we had on, found to our satisfaction that there is no fun in soldiering.

As she read the tiny inked script, it was as if she could hear his voice speaking the words.

September 10th

All hands are in line fully equipped with forty pounds of cartridges in our boxes and fifty pounds of knapsacks, rifles, and canteens on our shoulders. We remain in ranks, holding up our loads and pondering on why we aren't on the move. We forgot that great armies led by great men must accustom themselves to learning things gradually or they might not rightly appreciate them.

Back home he was perhaps a newspaperman or a teacher like her father. He obviously wasn't just a farmer who'd become a common soldier.

October 9th

Rain—rain—rain. Rain in showers, rain in torrents, rain with all its changes, with every variation to render it interesting. Cooking in the rain, eating in the rain, almost sleeping in the rain. When the rain had saturated us to the skin, it ran in gurgling rivulets down our backs, and those poor fellows who had no holes in their boots to let it out were compelled to carry double rations of water.

She looked up. Her eyes adjusted to the orange firelight, and she studied his profile.

What a pleasure it would have been to have a man like that around. Someone lean, chiseled, and noticing. The kind of man who actually saw the world and was amused by it, not the kind who merely plodded through the days not knowing, just doing what everyone else did.

She tried to visualize his wife. He'd have had his pick of any woman in his town, she was sure of that, and he could have swept off someone like Melissa Pruitt, the prettiest and most popular belle in Bentonville.

But, no, despite her prettiness, Melissa Pruitt had no understanding, and a man with his penetrating green gaze would never have married someone like that. Melissa had been chosen to give the farewell speech while she presented the colors to the troop, and she'd sent all the men—including her Nathaniel—off with tearful and patriotic bravery, assuring everyone in the town square that they were willingly sacrificing their loved ones for a sacred duty. Nathaniel, with his flat gold eyes that might have been cut from gourd rinds was one thing, but this Union man was something different. His wife would never have made Melissa's pronouncements. No woman on either side would have willingly allowed him to die on the battlefield, whether to preserve the Union or to save Southern liberty.

And she abruptly recognized a feeling of great sympathy for the wife from whom he was absent. The absence of Nathaniel—or Sy— might be an inconvenience, but to be apart from such a man as this was more than that.

She pulled her stare back from him to the diary.

October 20th

Our camp is in a field of ragweed so high and rank that you cannot distinguish a man from a horse. A stagnant pond close by, containing the half-decayed carcasses of mules, horses, and hogs is the water we must use. I saw many a poor fellow with swollen tongue and parched lips quench his thirst at this mire-hole. Others would fall back in dismay, sick at heart at the loathsome sight.

The room had begun to cool, and she got up, put more wood on the fire, and took her cloak from its hook to wrap around her as she sat back down.

November 1st

I don't know but that I think Iowa soldiers have been brought a very long way to do a very small business.

He was from Iowa.

Perhaps from a farm much like hers.

The wife back in Iowa would be watching for his return from a window much like hers. The woman would be doing what she did in the day and in the evening would be knitting him a pair of woolen socks. But of course she'd also have his children to attend to, for he was a man who would have fathered children.

She turned the little diary over to mark the place, took up the candle, and carried it to the bed. The candle flames showed the planes of his jaw, the laugh creases at the corners of his sleeping eyelids, the straight line of his nose.

She reached down and laid her hand on his forehead.

As her fingers stretched across his flesh, she quickly told herself that she was checking for a fever. His skin was warm, but not too warm, and he didn't flinch back from her palm, but took a relaxed sleeper's breath, as if he were accustomed to being touched in the night.

She felt her face grow hot at the pattern of her thoughts, and she crept back to the table and sat down, flustered. The candle flame wavered and flickered above the knob of melted wax as she righted the diary again and found her place. But she had to read the passage twice before her nervousness abated enough for the words to focus.

November 15th
We are camped by a battlefield and the rain is washing dirt from the bodies of soldiers buried here last year. We can't tell from the remains which army they belonged to, but as the skulls appear from the ground, we each hope that we will have a better grave than this.

Her eyes began to burn, but she read on with a sense of urgency. He'd be leaving in the morning, and she'd have no further chance to read his words and learn about the war. No further chance to know him.

She read about the skirmishes, the lack of food, the snow and the crossings of the White River that froze the men's feet. Yet among the bitter scenes, she felt a jolt of pleasure when she saw the names of her towns in his handwriting, Prairie Grove, Yellville, Fayetteville, spelled out in his neat lines, and it was as if somehow they were sharing those places.

November 18th
I have noticed many fine farms and orchards enclosed by worm fences and foundations on which stood fine residences, but everything has been burned and the fences broken and the orchards laid waste.

What a shame it all was. Trees like her apple orchard so carefully nurtured. Fingers plucking off withered leaves and worms, watering the roots through summer drought with buckets from the well, and then an army kicking aside the fences, felling and burning the trees in the sight of the woman who cherished them. And a handsome Yankee wounded, his shoulder so mangled that he might well lose the use of his arm. How sad and useless the waste of it all.

December 7th

Since twelve o'clock the battle has raged with fury. Our company, acting as skirmishers, took up a position in a cornfield directly opposite the enemy's battery. We lay low, for bullets flew thick around us and we seemed to be the main target for their sharpshooters. We had advanced nearer to the foe than we should have and were in danger of being cut off by the rebel cavalry. Then the Iowa Twentieth was ordered . . .

She turned the next page, then the others, but the rest were blank.

He'd stopped writing in the middle of a sentence the day before. He'd been writing about the gunfire at the same moment she'd been hearing it from her porch. He'd been describing what she'd been noticing even though they were miles apart.

And then his company had been ordered to retreat or advance.

She closed the diary and held it between her palms. It warmed to her hands and it was almost as if she were touching his forehead again. Holding his words was somehow like touching the eyes that had seen the events, like touching his forehead and his mind that had thought those words to write.

She shut her eyes and pressed the little book and felt that she was on the brink of a discovery about herself. About all women.

If a woman didn't know a man's thoughts, how could she love him? Unless she knew what he had inside, she was merely accepting what everyone else said she was supposed to honor—the appearance of strength or decency. But to get beyond the surface, to make up her own mind, a woman had to know the depth of a man, had to know the true strength that came from understanding.

But how was a woman ever to know that interior of a man unless she knew his words? And if the Yankee were a well man, would he be a talking man?

She was able to know his bemused view of life, his thoughts, because he'd accidentally stumbled upon her cabin and she'd been able to read what he'd written. But had his wife ever gotten that chance?

She looked up from the table.

Gray light filled the window square, and the fire had burned to embers without her noticing.

It was nearly sunrise.

She blew out the stub of candle and looked down at the diary.

How lucky his wife would be to have it when he got home.

She got up stiffly and tiptoed as quietly as possible over to the bed.

But as her eyes adjusted to the gray light, she realized that no matter how much noise she'd made, she wouldn't have disturbed him.

She forced herself to reach out and touch his forehead once more. The skin was cold, unresponsive, inflexible like paper. She carefully lifted the quilt. The bandage of torn sheeting was still in place, as pristine white as when she'd finished binding it. But he must have been bleeding internally. Even as she'd tried to save him, he'd been bleeding to death.

As she'd sat through the night, she'd never entertained the thought that he might die.

And yet he had.

When daylight reached her pasture, she'd walk toward the grove and find a Union troop that could deliver his body and his effects to Iowa.

His wife must have the little book. A woman could read, reread it and fall in love continuously with the man who had written the words. She knew that if she'd been married to such a man, how dearly she would treasure his diary and how grateful she would be to the unknown woman on the opposing side who had saved it and returned it to her.

She stood in her cloak beside the bed while the room lightened.

The December sun became pale yellow on the frozen windowsill, but no color touched his profile.

There was no use building a fire before she left.

Someone in the Union troop would know his name so that his wife could get the precious diary.

She didn't try to be quiet any longer, and her heels clacked on the pine boards as she walked away from the bed, took down her bonnet from its peg, and tied the ribbons at her throat.

She'd only heard him ask for a drink of water, only heard him murmur a few words as she bandaged his fatal wound, and yet she knew him better than she'd ever known any man.

She reached down and picked up the tiny book.

Then, before she realized she was going to move, she was bending down, opening her cedar chest. She held the lid with one hand while she reached between the layers of cloth and hid the diary between the folds of her wedding dress.

She stood upright again and carefully shut the trunk.

She gazed at the face of the man on the bed and took a jagged breath that in the cold air of the room sounded like a branch against the window.

Then she opened the door to the gray yellow morning and went outside.

Slave Quarters

"MISS AMY, Little Cicero bad this morning." Cleo's matter-of-factness reached through the haze of sleep and mosquito netting. "Miss Amy, Little Cicero some bad."

"All right! All right!" She turned over but didn't open her eyes.

If only they'd let her rest. If only they weren't constantly pulling at her skirt, hanging at her knees, dragging her into their quagmire of helplessness.

As her limbs awoke, she felt the ache in her arms, back, the more-than-dull pain in her right hand that had clamped the great scissors open and shut, over and over, open and shut, sawing through the coarse slave cloth hour after hour, cutting around the pattern for their fall shirts until the tracing paper shredded and her thumb on the scissors swelled double. She could barely raise her stiffened fingers to rub at her caked lashes. She'd worked until after midnight to finish the shirt pieces, and her eyes were protesting the strain of tracking the flimsy paper outlines in dim candlelight.

Couldn't they see they were killing her?

"What time is it?"

"It morning, Miss Amy."

She peered through the netting, but she couldn't distinguish the border between Cleo's chocolate face and her blue scarf. The two colors that should have been distinct merged in her tired sight, mingled without a definite line.

"Little Cicero, he bad."

"All right. All right," she repeated as she disentangled herself from the too-warm sheet and saw that the July sun already banded the carpet through the shuttered windows. The day would be insufferably hot.

Cleo had laid out one of her flimsiest weekday frocks, and although Evans was due back from Helena in the afternoon, surely she'd have time to go down to the quarters and return, change into something he'd approve.

She let Cleo dress her and brush her hair, let Cleo's clumsy fingers contain her curls in a slightly wrinkled everyday snood.

"You want the sick basket, Miss Amy?"

"All right."

She secured the ribbons of her straw bonnet. She was certain Little Cicero had a simple summer cold that would soon run its course, but the servants always felt more comfortable if she allowed Cleo to carry the basket with its lint, rubbing alcohol, and plantation-concocted cough syrup when she went to the quarters on a sick call.

Little Cicero had been running a slight temperature the morning before when he'd rushed up to her and she'd lifted him to reach a green plum, but his great dark eyes had been as sparkling and his grin had been as joyful as ever. She couldn't imagine anything more serious than an increased temperature, and she'd have ignored the distress of anyone but Little Cicero that particular morning when she was so tired.

"Tell Persephone I want my juice cold this morning. I want the fruit, the butter, the jam, everything cool but the muffins when I come back up to the house from the quarters," she said as she swept by Cleo and went down the staircase. "And tell Big Dido and Athena to start pinning those shirts together."

"Yes'm."

Whenever she gave a series of orders and ran through a series of the servants' names, she was made conscious of Evans's classical education. He insisted on naming each newly born or purchased house slave from his Greek or Latin books no matter how difficult it was on her to remember the pronunciation or how hard it was to get the recently acquired servants accustomed to the new names when they'd been answering to something more humble for twenty years. Evans didn't have to manage the house, and he never considered details like that.

Nor did he consider how they wore her down with their demands and their clamoring for attention, how they eroded her the way their constant fingering had dissolved the paint from the toes of the hanging Jesus in the chapel.

She was walking with dragging steps, but she still almost reached the slave hut where old Cassiopeia tended the small children before Cleo caught up with her.

"Little Cicero inside," Cleo said gravely. "Old Cass take the rest a them children down to the pond so they don't catch what he got."

She grimaced with tired irritation. Little Cicero didn't have anything serious.

But she was too fatigued to lecture Cleo, and without a comment she ducked inside the little cabin.

There was no window, and with Cleo blocking the light from the doorway, it was as if she'd plunged into a darkened theatre. If there had been any furniture but the bed in the room, she'd have stumbled, and as it was, she banged her knee on the wooden side. Her eyes took another few seconds to make out the form of the baby in the center of the quilt. She scooped him up and carried him to the door.

She'd never felt flesh so hot.

He blinked groggily at the light and rubbed his eyes with one hot dimpled fist.

Then his fevered eyes registered her, and he threw his arms around her, hugged himself against her. She felt his heat press into her bare neck.

"Take off my hat and go get a chunk of ice from the spring house," she ordered to cover her own alarm. "And don't dawdle and let the ice melt on the way back." She shook her snood free as Cleo removed the hat and placed it on top of the basket beside the door.

She didn't watch Cleo go as she began to hum and rock the child in her arms.

He held his soft baby cheek against hers and the dry heat of his skin seared her cheekbone.

But then as she swayed him gently back and forth, she felt the parching heat slowly evaporate. She drew her head back from his and smiled. "See, all you needed to get over that temperature was for me to come hold you." She stroked his hair with her palm. "You little rascal, scaring me like that just to get my attention."

He grinned, and his rows of baby teeth glimmered wetly like tiny grains of rice along his gums.

She caressed his head and felt his warmth turn clammy.

Abruptly, he began to shiver. His jaw quivered and his little teeth clicked together with the cold.

She knew instantly.

He had malaria.

She'd seen it before, that summer pestilence in which the fever soared, only to be replaced by a chill, the body alternately burning and freezing until either the organs or the disease gave out. Such a tiny frame as Little Cicero's wouldn't be able to withstand for long the violent lurching between the heat and the chills.

She retreated into the cabin and quickly pulled the quilt from the bed, wrapping it around him. "I'm here now."

But even as she tucked the quilt securely over his little legs, the chill began to abate, and his temperature began to rise.

She dropped the quilt to the hard-packed dirt floor, cradled him and kissed his cheek before the fever could obliterate the touch of her lips. In the dusk of the hut, her hand was the shade of his little forehead as she gauged the climbing fever.

She was almost certain Evans was bringing a fresh supply of quinine for the summer.

But could she risk administering even a small dose to so tiny a baby?

His arms draped over her shoulders, but he was no longer hugging her as the fever mounted. She held him close and carried him around the room.

As soon as he'd learned to take halting steps, he'd aimed his wobbling feet toward her, and not a day had passed in the previous year without his rushing to her, without her receiving his guileless embrace. She was always aware that the others were petitioning for favors, for treats, for intercessions in work schedules or punishments, but Little Cicero was too young to manipulate. His genuine smile and affection were for her alone.

"Miss Amy, Percy say breakfast ready." Cleo stamped up a feathering of dust in the sun-baked yard. "Here the ice. About freeze my hand bringing it, but I got it like you say."

"Little Cicero has the fever," Amy said.

Cleo instantly disappeared from the doorway.

"Lord, Miss Amy, put him down. You catch the fever, too. Put that child down." She raised her voice as she backed away from the cabin. "Can't nobody do nothing for the fever. Put him down. Old Cass be back later and check on him. Come on now, Miss Amy, and go back to the house."

The fever was extinguishing, and his teeth were beginning to chatter with the cold. The vacillations swung more rapidly with each surge and drop of his temperature.

"I knowed he shouldn't of eat them blackberries last week. Blackberries bring on the fever sure, and now we all going to catch it. Come on, Miss Amy, let him be."

"Give me the ice and hush. Then go up to the house and see if Mr. Reston's back yet. Tell him I said for you to bring me the quinine."

She decided she had to risk giving it to Little Cicero.

"Marse Evans don't want you down here where there's fever." But she nonetheless approached the door and extended the chunk of ice, by then no larger than a river pebble.

"Go on now. And run straight back with the quinine if Mr. Reston's home."

She carried the baby in both arms, sweating in the muggy darkness as she eased down on the husk mattress of the bed. Her muscles were going dead. Little Cicero lay limp against her shoulder, the terrible heat scalding through her sleeves.

He winced at the ice as she circled it over his little face and chest, but he didn't open his eyes. The melting dampened her bodice, but she disregarded the wet patches and pressed her cheek on his hair.

He was such a loving baby, his little face glowing with pleasure whenever he saw her.

She sat, her deadened arms supporting him by sheer force of will. She was so tired. They'd worn her away so completely that her strength was nearly too sapped to be of use to Little Cicero, the only being on the plantation she truly cared about, the only soul on the six hundred acres who wanted nothing from her but her presence.

The others all used her. Even Evans, so unconcerned about leaving her alone on the plantation that he never gave a moment's thought to her isolation. He said he'd definitely return that afternoon, but she knew that if some more entertaining distraction presented itself, he might delay another two days. And if he had a chance to cross the river and buy another Tennessee Walker or if he found a race to bet on, he might extend his absence for perhaps another week.

She patted Little Cicero, alternately retrieving the quilt and flinging it aside in his heating and chilling. His little tunic, of fragile cambric rather than the heavy cotton the other children wore, was soaked, but she hesitated to remove it.

She didn't know how long she'd been rocking him, how many times the fever, then the chill possessed his little body. Sunlight slanted obliquely across the threshold while she clasped him as tightly as she could, feeling the beat of his baby heart against hers, trying to persuade herself that his tiny face had relaxed between spasms of the disease.

She hummed, unable in her fatigue to remember the words of any lullaby as the fever claimed him again.

Then she saw the melon flush of sky beyond the tops of the shaggy cypress trees.

The day had passed.

Soon the dusk and the mist would rise, and the miasma would bring the infection from the river. But for now, Little Cicero lulled into ragged sleep, and she propped him tenderly against her chest to go to the door of the hut.

She should have told Cleo to bring a kerchief to bind her nostrils and filter out the miasma. She should have told her to come back down to the quarters whether or not Evans was home.

She stood in the doorway and looked out at the dusty path to the plantation house, but nothing stirred.

Not a wisp of breeze reached her, and she stood watching the sky as it stained red, then purple. The nearest trees flattened into unkempt silhouettes, and she could hear the drone of mosquitoes in the stillness. When Old Cassiopeia reappeared with the other children, she'd have her hold Little Cicero for a few minutes while she rested her arms. It was as if they'd turned to stone.

She found it increasingly difficult to see into the growing darkness, and she carefully shifted the sleeping baby. He was cool again, and his little shirt was almost cold.

Then she peered closely at his little puckered face.

She knew he was dead.

"Oh, Little Cicero," she whispered.

His final breath had been so imperceptible that he'd eased from sleep into death without her knowing. His little body hadn't been able to hold out for the dose of quinine.

"Poor little baby," she murmured as she slumped exhausted against the hut doorway.

A hand brushed her arm.

"I was a bit late getting back. Cleopatra told me you were down here."

She hadn't heard him coming through the dusk, and his unexpected touch loosened her partial control. Her back began to shake. She could hear the tapping of his riding crop against his boot.

"Cleopatra mentioned that Little Cicero was sick," he said. There was a brief silence before he added, "I guess the little fellow didn't make it, eh?"

She shook her head. Sobs crowded against her throat as she swallowed.

Leather slapped against leather. "That's too bad."

She tried to nod, but her neck couldn't manage even the gesture of assent.

"I know he was a special favorite of yours, but we can always get you another child to pet. You let Old Cassiopeia take care of the body now, and I'll have Pompeii build a nice little box to bury it in."

She wanted to shout at him to shut up.

He patted her shoulder. "Don't take on so. Come on now before the night mists carry the contagion this way. We'll get you another little boy. Juno's come up pregnant."

If only she could have cut off his insistence with the twisted leather crop that tapped out the words. But she knew she couldn't raise a hand to him any more than Cleo could raise a hand to her. She let the tears spill from her burning eyes onto the little head of the baby as the whine of insects supplanted his reassurance.

Waiting for Gideon Prince

THE FIRE SHRANK into itself, and in another few minutes, the tiny irregular flames would flicker out, would leave her in darkness and allow the chill to spread. But she didn't stir from the chair to throw on another length of juniper. She didn't have to look to be certain that more splits of cedar remained in the old ammunition packing case she used as a wood box—she always counted exactly how many logs she had of an evening, how many were left for the morning to edge out the night cold—and she had enough to build up the fire.

Yet she sat motionless. She merely watched as the wood broke into embers, fell from the hot red center, and collapsed into a gray sift of ashes. She sat, seemingly unaware that the room grew colder or that her hands on the battered arms of the chair ached, colder still, as she waited.

Something bumped the door slats, and she raised her head, stopped her breath to halt the wheeze in her throat.

The gentle thud came again, and a dainty hoof tapped the porch boards.

It was one of the goats alerting her that it wanted in out of the cold.

She strained to listen to something beyond the little goat, but at last she turned her stiffened neck back toward the fireplace and the blackened wood with its last scarlet tracings.

"There was no need to go out that door, Arvel," she said.

The mottled stones of the fireplace had stood the same, the fire burning low, almost going out in the same timid way the night she and Arvel had sat waiting for Gideon Prince. There had been an identical cloudy sky blotting the stars, darkening the hard-packed ground around the house, and a wind had clacked the brittle hickory branches. That night a calf, rather than a goat, had come onto the porch. That night Arvel had got up clumsily and stacked another log on the grate when the flames sank down, and they'd watched the fresh log smoke and send out tiny darts of fire from the bark, as if seeing the wood catch was the only important thing they had to do.

Once she'd tried, "Maybe you ought to think about giving it up, letting it go," but Arvel hadn't looked at her, hadn't indicated he'd heard, and she'd dropped it.

Arvel was no great shot, and Gideon Prince would bring half a dozen hands with him anyway.

A thousand meager fires was only three years worth of nights, and she'd stared into twenty times that many fires since that night.

"But there was no need to go out that door," she said again into the icy darkness.

Arvel's single declaration had always been, "It's mine. From the White River to the bluff. President Buchanan deeded it to my pa." And his gold-bead gaze would follow the slope that carried the topsoil down to the level fields below, the only growing land on the stony place.

"But you ain't your pa," she'd said, and the gold-colored eyes had swung back, showing their eyeballs red woven with miniature threaded veins. That was the first thing strangers remarked about Arvel, the thing that caught their attention whenever he looked directly at them—half the time making them forget what they'd been saying—

those bloodshot eyes of his like yellow eggs in a red bird's nest that never seemed to clear up.

The red and gold of his eyes showed even in firelight, and when she repeated, "Remember, you ain't your pa," he looked as if he might answer, as if he might take offense at the implication he wasn't half the old man who had held off bushwhacker after bushwhacker, single-handedly for three years, until his heart had finally stopped, on its own, while he lay on his own shuck mattress.

But after a few seconds Arvel had glanced away from her again, without saying anything, without disputing that he indeed wasn't his father.

Arvel wasn't the kind of man to challenge Gideon Prince to keep his distance and then fire a warning shot from the window the way his father had done to caution the bushwhackers, and it was clear that he intended to step outside to meet Gideon Prince and his men, intended to stand on the porch in the shrouded moonlit night in full view of all the hired hands where Gideon Prince could gun him down any time he pleased.

"But he's got too much to lose now," she said, as if they'd discussed the possibility sometime during the hours they'd been waiting. "Maybe a few years back when he was starting over again, when he was striving hard to slap that brand of his on whatever he laid his hands to." She'd paused for a twitch or a muscle tremor from Arvel to show he was listening. That ridiculous brand Gideon Prince had to sear into everything he owned, a three-pronged fork—for the three converging creeks running through his pastures—embellished with the center prong fashioned into a P, "like something was caught sideways on your pitchfork," she'd commented dryly to him once, and he roared, his black eyes crimping shut with laughter, his dark hair flaring and flopping over his forehead.

"Maybe when the war was on and your pa died, he'd have come with a troop and just taken the land, but not now, not with the war ended and the state being back law-abiding and all. Gideon Prince—with all them medals for bravery—" she said sarcastically, "won't risk jail for a piece of bottomland on this side of the river."

"Colonel Gideon Prince ain't risking jail." His red-gold eyes reflected the fire. "He's got the legislature in his pocket. Him and his Devil's Fork Plantation are the law out here."

A juniper log had exploded, sprayed chunks of blazing embers around the sooted hollow of the fireplace, and when the silence dropped again, he'd added, "I got to defend what's mine."

"Is defending what's yours worth maybe getting killed over?"

He'd stared into the fire.

When the calf came up on the porch, they both jumped, having been listening for horses. Arvel got up in his ungainly way, and went outside to slap the calf off into the cedars. And later—she'd never calculated just how much later—when Gideon Prince had ridden up, she'd sat as she was sitting in the cold room and had let Arvel go woodenly out to meet him.

"I'm coming," he'd called, but not loud, as he'd hitched his rifle against his hip without sliding the spotted golden-egg eyes in her direction.

She'd listened then, too, and some of their talk had filtered through the wind that didn't allow her to distinguish individual words or individual voices.

Arvel had stepped off the porch, the conversation continued in the yard for a long time, and she'd sat and assured herself, "That's all they're going to do, gab out there in the dark. I didn't have to worry about him doing something foolish."

Then, almost as an afterthought, the two shots came.

Two distinct shots, close together, having none of the urgency such shots might be expected to have, being almost casual as if they hadn't really been important after all.

And then there was more conversation, and she'd waited, not getting up even when Gideon Prince came in the door.

"It was self-defense, Hadi."

He'd looked across the little room, and the fire behind her had played over him as if he stood in the middle of it. His leather boots, black leather belt, holster, and vest, his black eyes and swatch of black hair had flickered scarlet with the flames, and he stood shimmering against the night, mingled black and red.

"Is he dead?"

"It was self-defense, Hadi. He raised that rifle. My men saw it plain."

"You're a fool, Gideon Prince. You had no call to shoot him."

"He aimed that damned rifle right at my chest."

"You're a fool," she said again, the last words she'd ever spoken to him.

"You always was a damned fool," she said into the cold air.

The fire had gone out completely, and it was no longer possible to make out the darker mouth of the fireplace.

Even when Gideon Prince had deeded her the shack and enough land below the bluff to keep the goats, he'd had to do it through his foreman, an embarrassed man with a harelip that constantly grinned no matter what the occasion. "He don't have to give you this strip, Hadi. He bought the land fair at auction when you didn't pay the taxes, and he don't owe you a thing."

She'd only stared at him stonily from the porch, not looking behind him across the river and the trees at the vast green spreads Gideon Prince owned by then, as she'd held out her hand for the deed.

Three years later when Gideon Prince sent word he was dying and needed to see her, she'd said a flat "No" to that same foreman who'd gaped and grinned involuntarily. "But he's dying, Hadi."

She'd merely shaken her head, not repeating the "No" that might accidentally come out a "Yes" and bring her to look down into his devil's dark, glowing eyes.

The foreman had ridden away, sweat soaking the back of his shirt, and within two days more, Gideon Prince was dead.

Everyone in Fayetteville and Bentonville—even some of his former troop coming from as far away as Batesville and Pocahontas—had gone to the funeral, but she hadn't, telling herself that Rachel might hold the services with an open casket, being one of the Beltings, who did that sort of thing, all pomp and show and no feeling or substance. "Which is why Rachel Belting Prince couldn't keep her husband at home in the first place."

People came by, one, two at a time, to describe the ceremony and the burial, telling her how the Lieutenant Governor had attended and said some remarks about Colonel Gideon Prince being such a valued man in the state. And she'd listened and nodded as if it wasn't important.

For a while she crossed the ford and went to the graveyard, out of sight of the big house, to gaze down at the headstone with that same ridiculous pitchfork brand carved into it—the only thing Gideon Prince owned at last—but after a few years, briars and thistles choked out the plot, dirt sifted up, finally obliterating everything but the curve of the stone and the incised GIDEON PRIN, and there seemed little point any longer in hiking over to look at it.

That was about the time Rachel and his boys moved away, and as she sat in the tiny shack below the bluff, people came by to tell her about the grand furniture being sold out of the big house, about parcels of land being bought up one at a time, and then more of them at once, until at last the final section went to a railroad company. "I hear, Hadi, they figure on laying track right along the river, making the house a hotel for trainmen," and she'd nodded.

"That's what it come to," she said, as she'd said it many times before as she'd sat in the darkness. "That's what all your land-grabbing and your self-defense killing, and all that branding of what you thought you owned come down to, some trashy railroad hotel," she said, but she'd said it so often that no heat remained in the words any longer.

"I remember the night you even laughed about putting that brand of yours on me," she said. Since she rarely voiced that memory aloud it came out stronger. "That first night we lay together beside the spring. I'd like to see you try that kind of nonsense, Gideon Prince." Her tone was flat, but she smiled, then grinned outright, her old face puckering with the effort, her dry lips cracking in the black room.

"You always fancied yourself a rapscallion, thinking yourself such a man with the ladies, laughing, calling yourself the Prince of Darkness with your arms tight around me there under them trees full of green persimmons. But you always was a fool about any woman who could see into you and then stand up to you." She shook her head. "We was good together, you and me. But you had no call to shoot Arvel. He never knew."

But as she said it, the statement and its certainty faltered.

"Arvel never knew about us," she said again, testing it in the darkness, listening closely to her own wavering words.

Then she tilted her head.

She asked herself if Arvel had suspected and had gone out to get shot, defending his own, as he stubbornly said, because of her and Gideon Prince.

"Or is it just that it happened so long ago that I ain't remembering it right?" she murmured.

The scene rose with absolute clarity.

The two of them sat by the fireplace and waited. Arvel had gone outside and talked, the two shots had come, and Gideon Prince had walked into the shack to her that last time. And the final words she said to him echoed around her as if she were saying them aloud once more.

Gideon Prince hadn't been closed in like Arvel, guarding what he thought, or suspected, behind bloodshot yellow eyes, and disbelief had washed over his dark face as he'd stood in the firelight.

He'd watched her for a moment before the realization had flooded into his dark eyes, the realization that he could never return. And along with it came the certain knowledge that the killing had done it.

"We coulda gone on like before even if you bought up the land and Arvel moved away, if only you hadn't shot him," she said calmly. "I'd have done anything for you. You'll never know how I missed you since," she added as calmly, having said that many times as well in the black and solitary nights.

"This land was nearly worthless with that hollow running right through the smack center of it. And Arvel hadn't been worth shooting since he was nineteen years old. But you couldn't see that, could you, Gideon Prince? You couldn't see that all the killing was spineless, that sparing would have been more manly."

Her ancient hands lifted, dropped again to the arms of the ancient chair.

"But then, you always was a damned fool."

The Death of a
Confederate Colonel

*I*T WAS NEARLY the opium hour.

One of the doctors would arrive at nine, and Emily would measure out the twenty drops each soldier could have. She knew they were running low and that the opium tincture would be wasted on the boy whose stump was already granulating, but she would insist anyway, and the doctor would give in.

She glanced at the grandfather clock standing against the far wall of the ward.

8:35.

She poured water from the thick pottery pitcher into a row of cloudy glasses.

"—and I'm still angry that you didn't even write about your wound." The girl's voice took on a coquette's pout.

It was the blond girl who came in the evenings to sit with the young colonel who had lost his foot. A girl who was much too young and much too pretty even to be in the ward and who could never pretend to be one of the plain, over-thirty, and married nurses. This evening she wore a pale pink gown festooned with silk flowers, and pink ribbons that gathered her golden curls in a silken hairnet. Her dainty rose-colored slippers twinkled beneath her hoop as she sauntered up and down the aisle and talked to the wounded colonel.

"It wasn't a serious wound," the young officer, the youngest colonel in the Arkansas Fourteenth, by the name of Boland Miller, protested happily. "I was having a perfectly splendid time just before I got hit in the thigh. It was only a nick, but it knocked me flat." He spoke with a mixture of chagrin and merriment. "And before I could get up, something banged into my foot. I thought somebody tripped over me in the advance, and I didn't know until they picked me up that the cannonball had taken off my boot. But it never did hurt much, and I'm no trouble at all, am I, Mrs. Winthrop?"

She looked at him and smiled as she poured the final glass. Then she glanced again at the clock.

8:40.

As soon as a doctor came, she could leave. She felt dizzy with fatigue, and she remembered she hadn't eaten since morning.

"—so what I think I'll do is show you how fit I am right now. Let me hold your shoulder, and I'll walk a few steps for you."

Emily brought her attention back to the young couple.

Boland Miller was sitting up and about to swing his legs over the side of the cot.

The girl's pink skirt billowed in the candlelight and reminded Emily of an elaborately frosted cupcake.

"Colonel, I don't think you should get up until the doctor comes and tells you you're sound enough to—" she began as she walked toward him.

But he stuck his legs straight out with the expression of a happy toddler. The thick white bandage on his stump and his remaining foot in its thick gray sock were almost the same length.

"I think you should wait," she said.

"Now, Mrs. Winthrop, you know I'm one of the healthiest amputees in this whole hospital. I'll probably be discharged by the end of the week." He raised himself, balanced on the socked foot, and when the girl stepped to his side, he threw his arm over her shoulder. "And with the prettiest crutch in town—" He winked at Emily, "I could almost go dining and dancing at The Eagle House tonight."

"Why don't you wait another few minutes? A doctor will be coming in just a—"

"Watch this, Mrs. Winthrop." He looked from Emily to the girl, who was smiling at him the way she would have smiled at a schoolboy walking atop a fence. "I'll lean my weight on you for a second and then hop this leg forward. Ready?"

"Ready."

She was a tall girl, almost his height, and Emily could tell she'd be able to support him.

"OK. Now!"

He pressed against the girl and gave a short jump.

"See that, Mrs. Winthrop. I told you I was ready to go dancing."

He leaned on the girl and hopped again.

But as his foot touched the floor this time, he screamed a high, short scream. His arm flailed loose from the girl, and he collapsed across the cot.

"Oh, God!"

"What is it?"

Even in the dim candlelight Emily could see the crimson stain that burst instantly on his nightshirt as if someone had thrown a fistful of red dye at his leg.

"What is it?"

"Oh, God!"

His eyes twisted shut, and he grasped his thigh near the bloodstain as another gush of scarlet poured into the material from the underside of the cloth.

The girl tried to maneuver his head onto the pillow, but he screamed again. "No! Don't."

His fist clutched harder at his leg, but more blood spread. The cloth seemed to have dissolved into it.

Emily hurriedly laid back the sodden cotton.

Above Boland Miller's knee on the inside of his thigh, blood gurgled in a mounded fountain that sank, then bubbled again. His leg wound that had almost healed was obviously open again, and his blood was pumping through the gash.

Emily dropped the soaked cloth of his nightshirt, and without willing it, plunged her hand into the blood fountain. Her fingers sought the line of the cut and dipped through it. The thick red liquid and the muscle that closed on her fingers were warm. She felt the bone and the cul de sac of the wound. His heartbeat pulsed out another spout of blood, and she pressed hard.

He moaned.

But the geyser of blood didn't spurt again. Her blind fingers must have stoppered the artery.

"Go see if the doctor is coming yet," someone said, and Emily didn't realize she was the one who had spoken until the girl backed away down the aisle toward the door. Emily caught a glimpse of the pink gown splattered with crimson blossoms that for an instant glistened like red silk roses.

She looked down at the young colonel. Both his legs, the shirt, and the cot were bathed in blood, but no new stream was feeding the scarlet pool.

"The doctor will be here in a minute," she said. "We've got the bleeding stopped."

He opened his eyes by measured degrees and cleared his throat. "I guess I did get up a little sooner than I should have."

She glanced away from his face to see the plump black coat and vest of the doctor, who reached the side of the cot and scowled.

"What's going on here?" His red face peered at Boland Miller. "Get some water to wash this wound so I can see something. And bring some of those candles over here."

Two ambulatory soldiers came near the bed with tapers they'd taken from the wall sconces. Another of them carried the pottery pitcher of water.

The doctor frowned at Emily. "What do you think you're doing? Take your hand away from there." He brushed at her with the motion of shooing an insect.

"His artery may be cut."

"I'll be the judge of whether or not there's damage to an artery." He put his hand on her wrist.

But she tensed her hand, and he glanced at her, surprised.

As he grasped her wrist more firmly, she clamped the nails of her other hand into his fingers. "He may bleed to death."

The doctor's scowl furrowed deeper into his brick-hued forehead, and he may have flushed a darker crimson, but the light was too uneven for Emily to be certain. He nonetheless pulled his hand back as he said angrily, "Pour some of that water over this leg so I can see. Hold those candles closer here."

Emily was conscious of the water that ran cooler than the flesh and muscle around her hand, conscious of the thinned blood and water dripping through the canvas of the cot onto the floor. The doctor's thick shoulder brushed against her, and she could feel without seeing it that his hand beside hers was separating the folds of the wound as if they'd been the flaps of a pocket.

Her pulse beat into her head, and she realized she was holding her breath.

"Mm-m-m-m," the doctor hummed.

His cheeks puffed and deflated, and Emily felt his plump fingers exploring the interior of the wound as if the thigh had been detached, laid out for study.

The candles, so close that she felt their heat on her face, sputtered, and the pendulum of the clock ticked loudly.

At last, the doctor withdrew his hand.

He flicked a large red bandana from his coat and wiped his fingers, removed his pinkie ring, which Emily hadn't noticed he'd been wearing, and polished the blood from inside the band. The blood didn't show against the red of the bandana.

"It's too deep for anyone to operate," he said in a low voice.

"What does that mean?"

He didn't look at her or at the colonel as he put the handkerchief back in his pocket. "It means that the shattered bone wasn't healed and has snapped. It severed an artery."

A solemn tick sounded very loud, and Emily couldn't decide if she was hearing the grandfather clock or the measured drip of water and blood from the sodden cot. She realized that her fingers had gone dead with the pressure.

"It's too deep inside the muscle for us to be able to sew it up."

"Perhaps when Dr. Samuels gets here—"

"He'll say the same thing." He carefully adjusted the ring back on his finger.

"But he could give an opinion."

"Dr. Samuels has gone to Fort Smith," he said almost smugly. "He's part of the medical team examining General McCulloch's body, and he won't be back for days."

Before Emily could say something about doctors tending the dead rather than the living, Boland Miller interrupted. "How long do I have to live?"

The doctor looked at him severely. "As long as Mrs.—" He paused to come up with her name. "As long as Mrs. Winthrop holds her finger on the cut."

Boland Miller may have nodded, or it may have been the candlelight that gave the illusion of a nod.

Emily's entire hand had lost its feeling.

She glanced up to see the ruined crinoline skirt—the blotches already having turned rust brown—the round red face of the doctor, and the nightshirted soldiers holding dripping candles.

She couldn't distinguish the tick now through the thudding inside her head. Had someone stilled the pendulum of the clock?

Her hand had deadened to the elbow. She couldn't seem to pull enough air into her lungs.

Perhaps Dr. Samuels would be back from Fort Smith sooner than anyone thought.

Could she stand beside the bloody cot with her finger corking the colonel's blood until he returned?

"Mrs. Winthrop."

She heard her name as if someone had whispered it from a long distance away.

"Mrs. Winthrop, I guess it's all right for you to remove your hand now."

She focused on his face. The animation and the color were gone as if they'd been the first parts of his body to drain away.

"No, I—"

"It's really all right, ma'am," he said faintly.

"I—I can't."

Yet as she said the words she felt herself sway. Black squares began to edge in from the corners of her sight, began to multiply and merge.

She tried to blink them back.

She had to keep her numb fingers in place or Boland Miller would die.

She tried to concentrate on standing, but she wasn't certain her shoes were on the bloodied wooden planks of the floor.

The checkered blackness accelerated, flowed across her vision. The darkness thickened and swallowed her.

She didn't feel herself fall.

The Mistress

*A*S FAR AS SHE COULD SEE down the archway of oaks nothing moved in the lane. She let the curtain fall shut, tugged at the tie of her wrapper impatiently. The afternoon was turning warmer, and she could already feel her curls sticking damply to the nape of her neck as she opened the door to the hallway.

"Effie, have your heard Napoleon come back from Van Buren yet? He should be bringing a crate of books Lindsey's is holding for me."

"No, Miss Judith. He ain't come yet."

Of course she knew he hadn't, and she heard with satisfaction that Effie's sleepy voice came from the sewing room where she'd sent her with Piney to sew seed pearls on the new ball gown. But as she retreated into her bedroom and shut the door, the momentary satisfaction evaporated, and she made two irritated turns upon the carpet while she patted her forehead with a kerchief.

Any second she'd have to repowder her face, redo her hair.

Where was he?

It shouldn't have taken that long to go to Lindsey's, load the box into the carriage, and return. She'd ordered him to take the carriage rather than the heavier, slower wagon, so he'd be back sooner. She could count on Effie and Piney threading the tiny pearls for about three hours, but not much longer. She was well acquainted with their attention span.

She dabbed with the dainty handkerchief, blew a puff of air across her upper lip, and pulled aside the curtain again to stare at the empty alleyway through the oaks.

The irregularly splashed sunlight, the pattern of the shadows looked exactly as it had moments before.

She could have smashed the water pitcher against her table with vexation.

Where was he?

Then, just as she was about to drop the curtain again, she saw the carriage.

The bay, whichever one it was, stepped briskly through the alternating light and shade, and from the window, she could see the silk of Napoleon's hat twinkle as it moved through the patched sunlight.

At least he wasn't dawdling in the driveway even if he had on the road back from town. But she watched with no lessening of impatience as the horse reached the circular bricked entranceway. Napoleon reined to a stop and jumped from the still vibrating carriage just as Daniel sauntered into her view from the direction of the stables.

She could hear Napoleon's voice without being able to distinguish what he said as he gave instructions to Daniel, handed over the reins, and shouldered the box of books.

She aligned the ecru lace of the curtain at the side of the window and walked across the carpet with deliberate steps. She was suddenly very conscious of her thin slippers. She reached the door and opened it as Napoleon's boots rang on the final stair.

"Bring the box in here," she said loudly. "I want you to help me unpack and shelve the books."

"Yes'm."

She stood aside to let him pass.

"Put them over there," she ordered in the same loud voice as she shut the door and waited with her hand on the knob. She watched him keenly while he lowered the crate. "I thought perhaps you had trouble in town."

"Old Lindsey left the box in his shed. We had some time finding it." He flexed his arms, removed the black silk hat and rubbed his palm across his cropped hair.

She noticed his long, slender fingers with their nails the pale rose of oleander petals. "Did you wear a shirt under that coat?"

"No, Miss Judith." He gave a quick grin, and the startling white of his teeth appeared and vanished with the brief smile.

She walked over to him, close enough to detect the lingering odor of the stables, the faint wool steam from his livery frockcoat.

"Good," she said. She reached up to unfasten the brass buttons of the frockcoat.

She slowly worked the brass discs through the buttonholes, exposed the dark tendons of his throat, the dark curve of his collarbone, the rounded muscle of his chest that rose with his breathing just below her fingers. She consciously and deliberately delayed as she looked from his smooth glistening chest to the dark eyes watching her.

When she released the final button, he shrugged off the coat and dropped the heavy wool around their feet. He stared unwaveringly into her eyes and slowly raised both hands to her face. She inhaled while the heels of his palms cupped her chin, and the narrow fingers radiated beside her cheeks, temples, slid through her hair until their length framed her skull.

He leaned down as he tilted her face upward, and his lips pressed hers.

She closed her eyes, felt herself floating, being carried toward the four-poster bed. She thought she heard him whisper something, but she couldn't be sure as he sank down over her into the feather mattress.

Afterward, she lay on his outstretched arm and studied her pale fingers at the hollow of his chest. She couldn't powder the freckles on the backs of her hands the way she could disguise those across her cheekbones. But, of course, by then the powder would have melted away, and the orange tack-head spots on her cheeks and forehead would be visible again.

Did he notice them?

If he saw them in the afternoon light through the ecru curtain, how did he feel about them?

Did he have a slim, coffee-colored girl waiting in the quarters? A girl whose hand would have shone with a golden glaze? Would he prefer that shimmering sunlight warmth to her own blue-white skin?

He lay observing the carved flowerlets of the ceiling over the bed as if he'd never seen them before.

She twisted her head on his arm, felt her hair cling to the sweaty inner curve of his elbow. She swallowed the clot of anxiety, touched her finger to the tip of his nose with attempted lightness. "What are you thinking?"

His maroon irises swung toward her, and his arm curled over her shoulder to draw her against him. He smiled the brief smile. "Nothing."

But she was abruptly afraid he'd sensed her doubts and had held her close almost patronizingly.

"It isn't just because I'm the mistress, is it?" she blurted.

"What?"

She quickly covered his mouth with her pallid hand. "Nothing. Never mind."

She angled from his arm and propelled herself over the edge of the bed.

She thrust her feet into the thin-soled slippers and wrapped herself in the dressing gown without looking at him. "You better get dressed and open that box before Effie comes to the door."

He got up, and she felt him come up behind her, gently lift her hair and loosely clasp the back of her neck with his hand. "Yes'm, Miss Judith," he said softly.

She poured a glass of tepid water from the crystal pitcher and sipped it while she watched him collect his scattered clothes and pull them on, watched him effortlessly pry the wooden lid from the wooden crate.

When he finished, he stood up and approached the little table.

He stopped with his thigh at the piecrust rim. He flattened his palms on the waxed tabletop and leaned across the table to kiss her finger that held the tumbler. "If you going for a drive this evening, Miss Judith, I best dust them coach cushions."

She arched her shoulders but didn't move the hand holding the glass. "I'll send Sam to let you know if I decide to go out."

"Yes'm, Miss Judith."

He straightened, picked up the silk hat from the mantel, and went to the door. As he opened it, he repeated, "Yes'm, Miss Judith," as if she'd just issued an order, and pulled the door shut after him.

She stood with the water glass in her hand and strained to hear his boots on the stairs. But the runner and the great vault of the entry hall muffled his step, and she couldn't tell when he arrived at the front door.

He was already crossing the veranda when she got to the window.

Daniel waited beside the porch, and she saw him exhibit the bridle as his hand fanned the air and his mouth moved. Then she saw Napoleon smile, and she heard the murmur of his answer.

He stepped off the porch and walked with Daniel toward the stables. He was still talking, his long, lean hand gesturing as they rounded the corner, out of her sight.

Was he telling Daniel about his adventure of the last hour?

Or had he already bragged to the others before?

Did the whole quarter of servants know? Were they all slapping their knees with hilarity whenever Napoleon harnessed the bay for a carriage drive?

The shadows in the vacant lane may have been more elongated than when she'd examined them before, but she couldn't be certain.

She smoothed the curtain down once more, and the rust freckles on the back of her colorless hand seemed larger, more numerous than she'd ever seen them.

The Return

August 6

There's been no rain for weeks now, and the pond is a sluggish green already. It's actually almost a blessing to be without the horses, which were confiscated last fall.

We heard that Braxton's troop was engaged in another skirmish last week but that the Yankees were solidly beaten back. The Yankees are no match for our boys who were raised on horseback. Braxton always rode through the river when he came, and I can picture him in the sunlight waving his hat at me while I waited for him on the veranda. No one can handle a horse better than he can.

August 7

The fight outside Petersburg where Braxton is wasn't just another clash along the trenches, but was a terribly bloody battle and a great victory for Lee. The Union troops are always forced to give ground, and they always have twice as many casualties as our boys. After a battle in the spring, Braxton wrote that the Union dead were so numerous they seemed a blue carpet on the field. But Grant has so many men.

We know we have RIGHT on our side.

But of course the Yankees have unlimited resources on theirs.

August 8

It's barely daylight, but it's too hot to sleep, and I'm sitting here by the window to catch what little breeze there is from the veranda.

This dreadful war's been going on for so long, and Braxton's been gone for so many months that I can no longer see his features. I can only visualize him clearly when I remember him doing something.

I can see his tall, lanky form relaxing on a blanket, his lean hand pouring champagne into the crystal goblets he secreted in the picnic basket when Lysander wasn't looking. I remember his beautiful slender hands on the reins, on the handles of his gleaming pistols, those strong, tapered fingers curved over his guitar strings, commanding our piano keys. He's so musical that it bothers me to hear anyone else play the piano. No one has his touch.

Mother warned me that he'll undoubtedly be out of practice, but I reminded her that he took his guitar, and I told her it's still as if the music in our parlor is awaiting his return.

August 9

Mrs. Littlejohn's son Jesse is here from Richmond, convalescing from a fever, and we had mother and son over for tea—steeped dried blackberry leaves, of course, but served with a fine biscuit that used the last of our flour. He's a captain like Braxton, and I imagined that his battle-stained uniform was Braxton's. I think that if I saw a Confederate officer with a new uniform now, I'd be quite certain he'd been hiding for the last three years. I'd be quite certain he was a coward.

Jesse said that the battle around Petersburg was fierce and one of the most appalling defeats of the war for that bungler Grant. And then he told how the Richmond ladies are valiantly coping with shortages by spinning all their own cloth and knitting their own slippers. He related an amusing anecdote about the servants in Richmond who despise the Yankees for shelling the town and interrupting their work. The servants get terribly irritated when they have to go into the shelters they call the "bum shelters."

Jesse is amusing, but he's every inch a planter's son and can't do a thing with his hands except hold a wine glass or a teacup. I'm glad I'm engaged to Braxton, who isn't that helpless.

August 10

More details filter in every day about that Petersburg battle. The Yankees tunneled under the trenches and used dynamite to blow a huge hole in our defenses. (Mother was infuriated when she heard that—"Men are supposed to fight standing face to face, not burrowing underground like snakes!") But after the Yankees had exploded their dynamite, they delayed too long, and Lee got his guns in position to shoot down into the crater as the Yankee troops ran across. It was as if our boys were shooting fish in a barrel, and I thought when I heard about it how awful Braxton would have felt having to kill men that way. He's such a good shot that he never would even aim at a standing deer.

August 11

I've been helping Sheba pick grapes to make jam for Braxton's return.

I don't know what he'll spread it on since flour is running forty dollars a sack now—when you can find it—but he'll like the fact that I helped select the grapes and directed the jam-making myself. I wore my new woven straw hat in the grape arbor, and it looks charming on me even if I do say so myself, and even if I did plait the straw myself. Braxton will love it. He's forever chiding me because I'm all thumbs, and he'll be pleased to know that I can do some things after all. I'm glad he's so capable of making and fixing, even to repotting plants and showing his servants how to graft trees.

I think he can probably do anything he sets his mind to.

August 12

Mr. Brent says he heard that the Yankees were using Negro troops at the Petersburg battle and that the carnage in the crater was the most horrible anyone has seen in this war. Jesse Littlejohn may have known about the slaughter, but he would never have related any gruesome details to us over our porcelain teacups. Sometimes I do get annoyed at the gentlemanly scruples that keep men from telling us things we really ought to know merely because those things are unpleasant.

August 13

I have a note from Braxton. It was actually penciled by a nurse in the Petersburg hospital and it says that he was wounded in the dynamite blast. He says he'll be coming home as soon as they let him travel.

He had the nurse, a Mrs. Dalrymple, add a postscript that he'll understand if I no longer wish to marry him since he wasn't wounded when I agreed to be his wife, and that he'll therefore release me.

How beautiful he is to think like that. He would, of course, be so noble as to make such an offer.

But I wrote back immediately, sending my reply with the same soldier who brought the letter, and assured him—my assurances looking much too feeble in pen on paper for what I was actually feeling—that I had no intention of releasing him.

August 14

Any belle who has the chance to wed a brave wounded soldier is the envy of all the girls around, and I don't know of any girl in the entire South who would be so base as to refuse a returning hero.

I feel deep down that Braxton will be coming home to stay, and I can't express on paper how glad I am that he'll be here with me and far from the horridness of this terrible war.

August 15

I wrote to Braxton and asked for details of his wound, but I hope he can be home before he has to answer the letter.

Since I can't picture his features, a scar on his face won't mar his image, so he needn't worry about that. And men are lucky enough to be able to grow beards that can hide almost any disfigurement of their jaws. They can handle the loss of an eye quite handsomely, too, and a man with a silken patch can stay dashingly intriguing while a woman would be merely loathsome.

General Hood lost his leg early in the war, and he was able to order a wooden leg from London that allowed him to do everything he'd done before—ride and dance and flirt outrageously at balls. I heard he was quite the ladies' man even on crutches while he was waiting for his new oak leg to arrive through the blockade.

That Mrs. Dalrymple is probably already more than half in love with Braxton. All my friends are. I should write her a nice note thanking her for taking care of him and writing his letter, but I somehow feel like waiting to see him before I do. I can't quite get myself to write it blindly. She may be a war widow, and Braxton may have become attached and attracted to her—which wouldn't be too far-fetched since she's there and would appear an angel in her mercy no matter how plain she is.

If he *has* become enamored, I'll be able to tell when he gets back and I mention her name. But I'd like to have that information one way or the other before I communicate with her.

August 16

I rather frightened myself yesterday with fantasies of that Mrs. Dalrymple, and I couldn't get down to concentrating on anything all afternoon.

Lindy was supposed to be helping me card wool, but since my mind kept wandering, I didn't watch her closely. Her excuse was that it was too hot to be working with sheep curls, but at any rate, the whole basket will have to be redone today.

What if Mrs. Dalrymple is a beauty and Braxton has fallen in love?

That happened to Em Curry. Her Richard found someone else within two months of being sent to Mobile. And the ladies around Petersburg will be even more stylish than the belles in Mobile. What if his offer to call off our engagement was merely his excuse to free himself so he'd be able to court the lovely widow? I can see her watching fondly as he convalesces and plays his guitar to cheer himself up. He took it with him to help with the boredom of camp life, but now he could be playing for her and singing all those gentle love songs he used to play for me.

August 18

Well, for two days, I've worried myself into near despair.

But now I've come to terms with any fears about that woman. If Braxton has found someone he prefers, I shan't hold him to any promise he made as he went off to war. He would of course be noble enough to marry anyone merely because he said he would. But he needn't do *me* any favors. If he wants to be free, he shall be. Neither of us would be happy if he wanted to be with someone else, and I'm not such a horror that I couldn't capture another man if I were in the market for one. Even Jesse Littlejohn with his happy-go-lucky attitude about everything seems quite ready to be smitten if I weren't already betrothed.

August 19

Another day, and I'm completely over the Mrs. Dalrymple scare.

Braxton wouldn't have phrased his letter that way if he'd been angling to get out of our engagement. He's much too honest and honorable to pretend. He'd simply have said he wanted out of the commitment. As it was, he was offering to let *me* go, not offering to run off with someone himself.

And the poor lady is probably well advanced into middle age anyway. I'm certain they don't allow attractive widows in the hospitals among all the wounded who have to be bathed and have their dressings changed. The very name "Dalrymple" sounds doughy, like it should belong to someone very round and plump and double-chinned. I'll warrant she's in love with him, especially if he's been playing his guitar, but I'm almost positive once more that he's not in love with her. He's been in love with me since he was ten years old.

I can hardly wait for him to be here. I can hardly wait to hold his hand and go gathering hickory nuts and black walnuts before the squirrels find every one of them the way they did last year. I think every squirrel in the country was searching out nuts on our plantation last fall, and Braxton is such an unerring shot that he can get basketsful of squirrels for Lysander to skin and Sheba to bake. And actually, a squirrel collar on that worn blue cloak of mine would do wonders for my morale.

How lovely it will be to have him back, to have music again.

August 20

How long ago was that beastly battle? How long will it be before Braxton can travel and be here with me again? He should have my letter by now. I keep hearing his strumming in my head, and every time I see one of the servants running across the lawn toward the house, I just know they're coming to announce his arrival.

August 21

The jams are simmered, potted, and stored away. I couldn't tell the difference between the molasses we had to use and the sugar we made jellies with before the war. But then perhaps I've become accustomed to substituting what the servants call "long sweetener" for scrapings from a sugar cone. I've certainly become accustomed to everything else in this interminable war.

How many weeks will it be before he's here?

If he'd succumbed to hospital fever or if something else had gone wrong, I feel certain that kind matron Mrs. Dalymple would have written me. And if his wound has healed and he's been sent back to the front, I do wish he'd write.

August 22

Jesse Littlejohn was back in Arkadelphia again this week, delivering dispatches, he says, but I suspect he came to see me. Why is it he can come and go with such ease when Braxton hasn't yet returned?

I'm thinking a late summer or early fall wedding might be wonderfully different. Everyone always plans weddings for June or Christmas.

August 24

I've been wandering around the house like a hot and restless spirit. How much longer before Braxton can come?

August 27

Braxton came two evenings ago. Both his arms are amputated at the shoulders.

August 28

His parents drove up with him in their buggy drawn by the only mule they have left.

I could tell his mother had been weeping, but of course she smiled and smiled and kept saying how glad we all are to have him back.

She said it so many times.

August 31

I worried about Mother, but she's the epitome of what it means to be a Southern lady. She patted Braxton on the cheek and said he simply must taste Sheba's corn muffins, which she knew he couldn't get at the front, and she kept popping bite-sized pieces in his mouth as if it were the most natural thing in the world.

September 1

It's one thing when the servants stare at the two empty sleeves, the cuffs pinned at the shoulder seams, but it's quite another when Em Curry can't take her eyes off them. She came to pay Braxton a welcome-home call, and I don't think she looked at his face the whole time we sat in the garden.

I can't remember when I've seen such a lack of tact. No wonder Richard found someone else.

September 2

Mrs. Brent is no better than Em Curry.

But then what can you expect from an overseer's wife?

September 3

We haven't talked about a wedding yet, but it's really too hot to think about much of anything beyond the possibility that the evening may be cooler than the afternoon.

September 4

The sky stays cloudlessly blue and the water in all but the largest pond has dried completely.

I've ordered Sheba to boil the rice in the early morning hours, but the resulting tepid rice is barely palatable by noon.

Braxton had his boy Jeremy cut some reeds to use for sipping straws, and he left a number of them here in the kitchen.

September 5

It would be harvest time now if we'd planted anything this spring. Perhaps it's just as well that Hannibal and Percy have run off to the Yankee lines in Little Rock. All they did the last two months was loaf and get in everyone's way. Braxton's Jeremy is an omnipresent shadow, and I do understand that he has to be nearby in case Braxton needs anything, but it's so hot to have him constantly hanging over the back of the chair.

September 6

No one has put by any crops.

I can't imagine what we'll do this winter without any meal. I know that, as the poem says, "To doubt the end were want of trust in God," but sometimes I can't hold out much hope that we'll ever be free of the Yankees.

September 8

Mr. Brent says that two more field hands have gone. But there's certainly no sense in sending anyone after them. We don't need two more useless mouths to feed.

The unrelenting sun is not only scorching our poor empty fields but is making ashes of my thoughts.

September 11

The Armstrongs gave a ball last night for their two sons who got furloughs together. Braxton said he wasn't recovered enough to attend a party, and I understood. Some unintentional rudeness is bound to occur when people try to enjoy themselves at a ball, and I understand that, too, of course, for, as it was, during one whole evening, we could forget the war.

The Armstrongs had saved all year and they served boned turkey and pound cake and ices just as if the Yankees weren't on our soil, and we really could blot out the war momentarily. Any time I was standing with a group and someone brought up the Yankees or even Marmaduke, I simply walked away. For six entire hours it was as if there wasn't a war or anything unpleasant. Even the night seemed cooler than usual.

September 12

What a lovely thing to have a ball to savor in my memory again.

The music was so sprightly and happy, and I danced and danced.

Jesse Littlejohn dropped by to return a glove he thought was mine. He wore a uniform more ragged than the one he wore last, and two of his buttons had "U.S." embossed on the brass. When he saw me looking at them he said he'd had to replace two he'd lost with either homemade wooden buttons or some off a Yankee uniform. He said he finally chose the brass ones because the duped Yankees didn't know that "U.S." actually stood for "United South."

September 14

Jesse can't seem to shake the fever he got at Chancellorsville. He came by this afternoon to bring Mother a paper of real coffee, and he said the Yankees were moving up the Shenandoah Valley and destroying it utterly. That's always been such a lovely valley, and Mother was shocked by the barbarity.

September 15

What dreadful heat!

Braxton came by this afternoon for the first time since the ball, but my images of the evening are so faded that I couldn't think of any amusing incident to tell him.

He's no longer wearing a uniform, and it's strange to see him in an ordinary homespun shirt.

September 16

We hear that as the Yankees get closer to Richmond there are no end of weddings.

It must not be this hot in Richmond.

I couldn't possibly plan a wedding in this heat.

The Confederate Wife

MIST LAY BETWEEN the pasture and the hill, a snow mist that ghosted the cedars, obliterated the gentle peaks that usually separated hill and sky.

Her breath panted in clouds of mist and she pressed her lips shut against the visible cold while she glanced around the icy room and took her coat from its peg. The ovals of the tintypes on the dresser reflected the morning light, and the likenesses of Isaac and Price in their uniforms became as hazed as the outside frost.

The coat she took from the peg was actually Isaac's that he said wasn't worth taking to camp since the wool hung too frayed to stand even one winter campaign, but she'd kept it anyway. Once she'd managed to darn the worst worn spots, it made a good enough wrap, and it had lasted through the first three years of the war just fine.

But as she shivered and yanked her arm through the sleeve, the tattered strands gave way and a long rent reopened in the wool.

As she looked down at it, despair abruptly closed her throat. Her jaw sagged, and the exhaled steam betrayed her sudden helplessness.

Why now? Why today?

She'd been planning ever since Isaac's last letter to spend the morning figuring in the book, counting, adding the new notes and the new totals without having to break off for some homely chore. She'd cleared away everything to make the free time. And here she was going to have to repair the ancient coat again.

She stared down at the rent for a long moment.

Then she tightened her lips and straightened.

There was no use letting something so trivial defeat her. It was just one tear, and she had some leftover butternut yarn that would hardly be noticed on the once-gray wool. She aimed to make Isaac's old shoes last until spring, and the old coat could as well. She wasn't going to spend good money for things that cost too dear already. The few remaining peddlers were asking outrageous prices, and she, for one, didn't intend to pay them.

She fastened the coat and clumped to the door. The shoes hung like wooden boxes on her feet as she maneuvered them off the back stoop. They were easier to wear in summer when they weren't frozen stiff. She pushed them clumsily along the iced flagstone path.

Icicles hung in foot-long glass spikes from the eaves of the barn, and the ragged edges of the shingles had smoothed into unrippled whiteness. The patches of ground snow were rock hard, and she knew it was well below zero.

She reached the woodpile, braced the awkward shoes, and began to load splits of oak onto one arm. The tear in the sleeve gaped under the wood's pressure, and her arm became instantly colder.

Next winter she'd give up the coat to gray squares for a quilt, but maybe the war would be over by then, and Isaac or Price would be home.

Her breath puffed loose in a startled cloud. Her temples thudded in surprise.

She hadn't meant to think that.

Isaac *or* Price.

She hadn't thought anything like that for three years. And she especially hadn't expected to think it while she stood beside the woodpile in below zero weather.

She grasped another length of oak.

But her distraction made her careless, and the oak log next to the one she grabbed was dislodged. Without warning, the top row of wood slid toward her.

The rolling two-foot logs of oak knocked her off balance.

She dropped the wood she held, and as the shoes skidded on the ice, she was slammed against the side of the barn. She fell on her back and flung one arm up to protect her face as the heavy oak crashed over her, around her, gouging and hammering her chest. The frozen ground vibrated as if the supports of the barn itself were collapsing on her. She was sure that at any second, a piece of oak, dense as a bar of iron, would crush her skull.

Then suddenly the wood stopped thudding down on her.

She held her breath and waited behind her clenched eyelids and upraised arm.

When no more logs moved, she finally opened her eyes. Her breasts, ribs, lungs felt battered, and she knew she'd be covered with welts and purple bruises by evening. From beneath her hand, she saw that over half the log pile had plunged onto her. She'd be a good hour or two tidying them into a decent stack again.

She started to lower her arm.

"E-e-e-e-e!"

The strange uneven sound rose aloft in a burst of steam.

It was her voice.

She moved the arm cautiously again.

"Ah-h-h-h-h."

A new pain careened into her head and the unexpected cry came again. She clamped her teeth and lowered her elbow toward her chest despite the chorus of moans it caused. When the arm rested at last against the two logs atop the gray wool coat collar, she saw through the beat of pain that the wrist hung in an impossible angle from the coat's sleeve. A chunk of wood had obviously snapped the bone. Maybe even more than one.

She watched her hand warily as she tried to sit up.

She couldn't move.

She turned her head slowly, careful not to jar the throbbing wrist. Her other arm and shoulder lay buried beneath a mountain of oak. She was wedged, pinned securely against the barn by the pile of logs.

She gasped in short spurts that coated her upper lip with moisture. It iced over instantly.

Pain welled from her marrow when she gave a tentative pull on the buried arm and shoulder. She stopped tugging, and her body shuddered.

She moved her head, unable to tell if the pain came from the shattered wrist or the imprisoned arm. No matter where the throbs originated, however, they engulfed her, and the black squares of dizziness checkered her sight. As she closed her eyes, the darkness turned to scarlet.

She tried to fill her lungs without moving, tried to unlock her tensed muscles and stifle the force of the pain.

Breathe. Relax. Breathe.

If she could dull the needle stabbings of the pain, she could think.

It ebbed, flowed, retreated again, a thing separate, complete, and in the trough of the next spasm, she opened her eyes.

A row of glass icicles hung just above her upturned face.

She had to plan.

Breathe slowly.

She'd think of something. She'd always thought of something. She'd made it on her own for years.

She alternately closed and opened her eyes around the waves of pain, but the next crest was too sharp for concentration, and she looked up, not thinking.

Points of ice hung over her like jagged crystal teeth.

Those first few minutes after she'd realized her mother wasn't coming back. . . . Breathe. . . . Those first few minutes had produced the same acute wrenching in her bones.

Breathe.

She closed her eyes, her mind, against that image from the past.

Remembering something that happened so long ago was wasteful.

What she needed now was to think about what to do in the present.

She recognized that somehow the pain had lessened. Was she getting used to it? Or was it only the first moments that were so terrible, like the first minutes of loss when she knew she was alone?

Perhaps frostbite was setting in.

She averted her gaze from the ice points while she avoided glancing at her wrist in case the pain might return if she saw it.

Her skirt and petticoat lay twisted about her knees. One of Isaac's shoes had skidded against the ice and lay, shabby and stiff, out of reach of her foot. She lifted her neck, and the movement jarred the pain into reality. She dropped her head to the snow again.

The panic of physical anguish was so similar to what she'd felt when she'd been five years old standing on her aunt's porch and knowing that she had been abandoned.

Isaac had never understood about the savings.

But Isaac and Price had never been abandoned. Neither of them had ever had to save all they possessed in order to know they existed. Isaac and Price and their sisters and their folks had been a family. How could any of them know what it was like to need to save, to conserve every morsel of food, every scrap of clothing, every coin and paper note?

That morning after she brought in the wood she planned to take out the money box and count the amount she'd saved since Isaac had left for the army. She'd planned to add his recent pay and to reckon the new total in the book. Neither Isaac nor Price could know the pleasure of handling the bills, could know the security of the crackling paper notes. She stacked the peach-colored bills one over the next, studied the undersides of the ten dollar notes that were pale blue and decorated like the backs of playing cards. She counted and recounted them, the hundreds of dollars of them. Every time she handled them, she knew she was rich.

After the war she'd have enough money even to afford Price.

Her eyes snapped open, and her heartbeat hammered through her skull, caused the pain to spear her again.

While she waited for calm to beat it back, she gazed at the ice darts above her.

The thought had ambushed her again.

Isaac *or* Price.

Both or just one of them might return from the war. And if Isaac didn't come back, she'd be wealthy enough, secure enough to marry Price. She'd saved enough of the colorful notes to afford, after the war, new dresses, shoes, a good warm coat, and Price.

She remembered the tear in the old coat sleeve with disengaged objectivity. She could no longer feel the cold, but then she couldn't feel her hip that pressed against the ice either. Was that frostbite, too?

The mist at the horizon had eased into the pasture, and from where she lay she could see that the outline of the house was beginning to blur in the advancing whiteness.

If it warmed a bit, it might snow.

She suddenly couldn't remember what Isaac looked like.

Was the pain, the cold disorienting her?

She could see Price's smile, his face that looked down on her as he touched her shoulder. But she couldn't call up Isaac at all. Not in his gray uniform or wearing the old gray coat she lay in.

The mist floated between her face and the icicles.

Her wrist would soon numb. When it deadened with the cold, she could push it against the woodpile while she pulled back with the buried arm. Then she'd be free. And the first thing she'd do would be to go into town and buy a dress. A pale blue dress the color of Price's eyes.

She almost smiled before she felt the ice across her upper lip, ice like glass.

All her life she'd saved, but perhaps now was the time to spend.

Price's sparkling eyes waited for her reaction to the six pieces of surprise molasses candy. Thick and dark and sweet and locking her teeth like the glass clinging to her upper lip.

She raised her head, and this time the pain remained in check. She looked at the mist-blurred house, at the egg-white stiffness of the frozen snow, at the legs straight before her.

She tried to move a foot, but the legs stayed clumsily inert below the wrinkled petticoat.

Her gaze followed the edge of the coat past the lattice of overlapping logs up to the sleeve and the broken wrist. She could see now that the bones pressed the skin taut, as if they were about to jab through, and she noted dispassionately how fragile bones were.

As fragile as the pink and blue Confederate ten dollar bills in the tin box. The box that would be as cold as the snow when she took it out of the armoire.

She slowly lowered her head, and the coat collar rubbed the back of her neck.

Price had touched her hair, had rubbed the back of her neck. If only she could have trusted that one day she would be wealthy enough for him.

She felt her jaw relax without her volition.

She could have floated away but for Isaac's coat and his remaining shoe that weighed her down.

She gazed calmly at the point of an icicle and let her mind dwell on the money a few minutes longer.

Then she admitted to herself that even if her wrist went dead, she wouldn't be able to move the logs from her shoulder, admitted that her mother wasn't coming back, admitted what she'd suspected as soon as she realized she was trapped beneath the wood, that lying below the crystal border of ice, she was going to freeze to death.

Bringing Travis Home

S SOON AS THE CLEAR AIR in my nostrils was overpowered by the odors of blood and rotting meat, I knew they'd sent me to the right place.

I swallowed hard a couple of times. A man, leaning in a chair balanced on its two back legs just inside the door, was looking at me.

"They told me this was the hospital." I pulled the letter from my dress pocket and unfolded it. "I came for my brother, Travis Woods. We got this letter from a Dr. Simpson that said we could bring Travis home."

The man waved an arm toward the far end of the building, which I could tell by then had been a church. "That's Doc Talbot up there. I don't know no Doc Simpson."

I looked where he was pointing. Rows of soldiers lined the floor so close together that it didn't seem as if anyone could step between them, and I'd have to walk the whole length of them to get to the baldheaded doctor he indicated. I felt self-conscious standing there folding up the letter, so I kept it in my hand as I started up the narrow aisle.

I stared at the face of each soldier, trying not to see the brown seepage on the bandages, trying not to see the empty spaces where legs and arms should have been. A few soldiers gazed back at me, but most of them just lay with their faces and eyes clamped in pain.

There was a constant rustling, gurgling, a sort of snore-like panting, and I didn't feel I was disturbing anyone as I clumped along the bare wood floor in my town shoes.

Autumn sunlight glared through the tall windows, and I found that the faces were all starting to look alike. What if I passed right by Travis and didn't know him?

I went by a soldier with a head bandage.

Travis had been gone so long, I probably couldn't recognize him by just a mouth and a chin, and I slowed my walk.

But then I saw that the soldier with his eyes and nose covered by a wide swath of bandage wore a Yankee uniform. He couldn't be Travis.

And I saw for the first time that Yankees and Confederates lay side by side, mingled on the rickety cots and on the floor. After I started separating out the blue and the gray uniforms, I calculated that maybe there were more blue ones on the cots than on the floor, but then the church *was* a Union hospital.

I got to the end of the long room where the doctor was standing at what had probably been the altar. He was scribbling in a ledger and he didn't glance up but said in an irritated voice, "What do you want?

I extended the letter. "I came for my brother. Dr. Simpson wrote that we could bring Travis home."

He looked up then, and his eyes were so blue, caught between his tanned cheeks and his tanned baldness, that it was as if they'd been assigned to the wrong face.

"Dr. Simpson was killed in a field hospital a month ago. You took your sweet time coming," he said, and the lids over the blue eyes thinned as he squinted at me.

"Pa had to get the harvest in before he could spare the wagon," I said to let him know I wasn't the one who did the deciding.

"It's always the same, isn't it? If some of these boys could get home in time, they might stand a chance. But there's never enough money to come get them while they could save a limb, is there? There's never enough time before harvest to take them home before they succumb to the fever, is there? Well, if Simpson said you take your brother home, I suppose better late than never."

"I looked at all the soldiers in here and I didn't see him."

He made an impatient gesture. "Well, if he improved enough, they might have sent him back into the battlefield to complete the maiming and the killing they didn't finish the first time."

"Travis was in the Confederate Army."

The doctor, who was about my height but stocky, peered at me sharply, not as angry. "Well, if we have a convalescent Rebel, the authorities may have taken your brother to a prison camp or exchanged him by now."

"Where's the prison camp?"

There was a pause as if he hadn't heard me. Then he said, "Or, in case your brother didn't get well, we have a temporary morgue out back where we stack the bodies until they're boxed and labeled."

The disgust and anger surged back into his words, but by then I knew they weren't aimed at me.

"Can I check there?"

His hand came to rest on the page, but he didn't write anything. "Do you have somebody to help you in case you find him?"

"Pa's boy, Archer."

"Oh, a slaveholding Reb, eh?"

I lifted my chin. "We've only got one."

"All right." He made the impatient gesture again. "I don't have anyone to send out there with you. Don't faint."

"I won't faint."

He gave me a long blue look. "All right. Go out this door. They're back of the shed. If we could find any identification on them, we put a note in their jacket pockets to tell who they were."

I folded up the letter and slid it my dress pocket. Pa would need it to show to some Yankee official to get Travis out of a Union prison.

I could feel the doctor watching me as I opened the door, but I didn't look back at him as I shut it behind me.

I walked around the side of the shed, and there they were, like the doctor said, laid out, not on top of each other in a pile exactly, but crammed together the same as if they'd been stacked, from one end of the shed to the other.

A dead animal odor drifted around them, but the fall cold hadn't hurried the decay, and the smell in the October sunlight wasn't half as bad as the stench inside the church hospital.

I walked along, keeping my skirt from dragging on their boots or on the socks of those who didn't have any boots.

Their faces were a stiffened yellow tan, a sort of murky uncolored-ness like cheap tallow, and they, too, all looked alike. The gray jackets, blue jackets, gray undershirts, trousers, were all so grimed and stained that I couldn't tell them apart either.

And then suddenly I saw Travis.

I knew him immediately, even among all the others he resembled, and I didn't need to check the slip of paper showing from his pocket that identified him.

I could see he had both his arms and legs. His face was all right with the eyelids slightly ajar and rim of white gleaming between the lashes.

I hadn't had any trouble recognizing him.

But there was something wrong with the way he looked. Not just the dead absence about him, or the narrow blank whiteness showing below his eyelids, but something else besides.

And I realized it was his hair.

Somebody had slicked it back away from his forehead. Mama would have seen it right away. She'd notice his hair the first thing when I brought him home. She was always so proud of his curls, saying, "What a shame that none of you girls got that lovely wavy hair," and adding, without meaning it, "What a shame it is to waste those beautiful waves on a boy."

I carefully wedged my shoe between Travis and the soldier next to him and leaned down to pull the hair loose from its unfamiliar pompadour.

His skin was cold, but yielding somehow, like day-old mush turned out of a pan. It felt almost moist, as if it had broken out in a sweat one last time.

I drew back my hand.

The hair hadn't fallen over his forehead in a curl, but was flared up, resisting and dead, more like arid grass than hair.

I didn't try to shape it again.

I reached over and took the cap off the dead soldier beside my foot and put it on Travis.

Neither one of them would mind.

Leaving
Gilead

1

SARANELL BIRDSONG HUNCHED on the top step of the porch and frowned.

"I don't care about the party, Madison," she said to the porcelain-headed doll whose cotton body folded on the step beside her. "Who wants to line up and be crushed near to death by dumb crinolines and sweaty gray uniforms just to get a raspberry ice?" Her frown deepened, and she finished bitterly, "But I didn't even get to wade in the river."

She'd pleaded with Renny as the carriage bounced across the ford, telling him the water had never been so low, not in any spring she could remember.

"And you being all of eight, too," he'd said in his mocking tone. "But you ain't getting in that river water in no town dress while you in my charge."

And he'd splashed the horses over the river pebbles.

Saranell now sat in a cotton play dress, clasping her knees with her arms as she said fiercely to the doll, "Papa should never have bought Renny. If old Ozra was still Mama's coachman, *he'd* have let me wade in the river."

Her father had in fact resisted when the slave trader, Early Yarborough, had brought Renny to the plantation, and without Saranell herself, Ian Birdsong probably wouldn't have bought that particular slave.

"I can tell that boy's got too much pride," he'd said. "I don't need no slaves on Balm-of-Gilead Plantation that won't take orders."

Saranell, only five at the time, had strolled barefoot along the grass, and as she'd passed Early Yarborough's wagon, the slave had glanced down.

His irises gleamed like persimmon jelly, and while Saranell stared into his eyes, he smiled. The smile had lasted no more than a second, but it had been genuine, and when the slaver had suggested that the

73

tall slave would make a good coachman for Mrs. Birdsong at the bargain price of only twelve hundred dollars, Saranell had said, "He's right, Papa."

Her father had glanced at her, and his expression altered at once. For Ian Birdsong, wealthy merchant that he was, trusted his daughter more than he trusted himself on matters of taste, and if there was anything hinting of elegance or class that Geneva Waverly Birdsong might possibly need or want, her husband would buy it.

"You think so, Saranell?" he'd asked, and when she nodded, he said, "If that boy can handle them matched bays of mine, I'll take him off your hands for a thousand even, Early."

Early Yarborough had called out, "You know how to handle horses, boy?"

"Yes, sir. I can handle horses." The man slid from the wagon bed and sauntered to the porch.

His cropped hair resembled black velvet, and his skin resembled the expensive chocolates Geneva Birdsong ordered from New Orleans. His plum-colored eyes stared at a spot of whitewash above Ian's head.

Ian Birdsong winced as he read from the slaver's creased bill of sale. "It says here your name's Renny. You born with that name, boy?"

"Yes, sir."

But his tone somehow lacked deference, and Ian winced again.

But he nonetheless signed the greasy document and had Saranell lead the new slave to the quarters beyond the kitchen.

Geneva Birdsong first glimpsed her new coachman the next day, and she'd laughed sarcastically. "Do you think he'll fit on the tiny driver's box of our old-fashioned buggy? I wouldn't be surprised, Ian Birdsong, if you didn't have to trade off that ancient thing and buy a new carriage to go with your new driver."

Her husband did, of course, order a new landau, the one that now waited at the curve of the driveway for Renny to return for him and Geneva after the gala military ball to which children had not been invited.

"What good is it for Papa to be a Confederate colonel and own a plantation and heaps of servants if I can't even wade in the river,"

Saranell complained. "You know, don't you Madison, that they'll be stuffing themselves on boned turkey and cream tarts while we eat stupid corn dodgers in the kitchen."

But her anger and bitterness had lost their force, and she sat only a moment longer before she jumped up, seized the doll around its cloth stomach, and trotted into the hall.

She stopped just short of the dining room threshold.

Renny had lit Geneva's new kerosene lamp, and he sat at the table in a puddle of golden light. His buttons glittered, and his skin glistened, but he was sitting so still that he might have been asleep.

He wasn't asleep, however.

His eyes moved rapidly back and forth as he looked down at the page of an open book beside the tea tray.

Saranell held her breath, then pressed her cheek hard against the doll's glass ringlets as she eased silently back down the hall and whispered, "Renny can read!"

She inhaled a deep and shivering breath in the dark before she let her bare feet hit the floor casually, as if she'd just wandered in from the porch. She strolled into the dining room and dropped into a chair across the table from Renny. "What are you doing?"

He glanced at her sharply and grasped the nearest polishing rag. "Them silver pieces for serving your mama's tea got to be buffed near once a week in this drought weather."

She waited a moment before she pointed at the book. "What's that?"

He scowled. "How many 'that's' you calculate in here? You think I about to keep track of every 'that' in this room?" He put aside the creamer and took up a pair of sugar tongs. "You suppose it might be a book somebody like your papa been reading?"

"What kind of book?" She could make out the upside-down title, *History of the Conquest of Mexico*, along the top of the page.

He glanced at her with an oblique glower. "How come you bothering me with them rattling-on questions? Suppose you ask your papa when he get home."

She opened her mouth, but he kept polishing the tongs as if she were no longer in the room, and she clamped her lips shut again.

The kerosene lamp hissed.

"Has Zilla got dinner ready yet?" she asked at last.

"You ain't crippled that I notice."

She sighed.

She waited another few seconds before she asked, "What time are you going back for Mama and Papa?"

"Near midnight. And you ain't going along."

She lifted her chin. "Who wants to ride in that stupid coach in the middle of the night?"

Before he could say, "You do," she slung Madison over her shoulder and hurried from the room. And as she went down the black hallway, she muttered, "It'd serve him right if I told Papa he was reading a book."

She stomped out the back door, but she halted on the brick path to the kitchen and her back sagged. "But the one thing Pap won't want to hear—" She sighed again. "—just before he's marching off to fight the Yankees, is that somebody already broke the law and taught Renny how to read."

2

SARANELL PROPPED HER ELBOWS on the plank table and watched Renny tilt molasses into a tin cup of coffee.

She'd just come from the front lawn where she and her mother had waved Ian Birdsong off in his gray uniform, and she still wore a Sunday dress and the white shoes and stockings Sunday dresses required.

She and Renny sat in the sunlit kitchen, each with a tin plate and a cube of cornbread before them on the table. Madison lay face up, her blue-painted eyes in her porcelain face staring toward the flies gathering along a crack in the ceiling.

Zilla, the plantation cook, had given them their lunch, and after admonishing Saranell not to stain the Sunday dress she'd just washed and ironed, had waddled away to her cabin.

Saranell didn't have a mug of coffee, and she sat watching the molasses, as thick and brown as the back of Renny's thumb, rise in a column from his cup. When he finally righted the jar, the coffee level had risen half an inch.

Her mouth puckered. "Do you like your coffee that sweet?"

Renny shaved the syrup edge with his forefinger and thudded the molasses crock onto the table. "If I didn't like my coffee that sweet, I wouldn't drink it that sweet."

He slid a tin spoon into the cup and stirred.

Saranell nibbled at a piece of cornbread. "You're not eating yours."

"Who can eat with that orange sun boiling down, simmering the eyeballs near out of a man's skull?" He stared moodily into the sunshine beyond the kitchen door.

Saranell tried another bite before she shoved her own plate aside. "Did you hear that Mr. Culver resigned from Papa's company and set sail for England?"

He nodded. "The grapevine spread the news that Mr. Ex-Major Haze Culver, husband to Mrs. Fanny Culver and owner of Rosegate

Plantation, done run off to London to sell his fine cotton and wait out this white man's war."

"Did you hear he took Mrs. Culver's maid Cassy to London with him?"

He nodded again. "London be good and cool this time of year with them hard rains washing all manner of dead rats and trash off the cobblestones."

Saranell stared at him with astonishment. "You've *been* to London?"

"Three, four times."

"London, *England!*"

"Captain Alphonse Phillipe René Thibidoux sail regular from New Orleans to London every spring."

"You've been to London!" She scowled. "I've never even been to Little Rock!"

He didn't glance at her, and after a moment, she asked, "Did you belong to that ship's captain?"

His head jerked and his eyelids thinned, and it was obvious he was angry.

But almost at once, sadness replaced the anger, and he said, "I guess you could say I belong, body and soul, to Captain Thibidoux, master of the sailing ship, *Atlantic Queen.*"

His thumbnail clicked the mug. "He always telling me he got them free papers signed and sealed. But the morning he drop dead crossing Dumaine Street, they don't find nothing but IOUs." He shrugged grimly. "And, of course, all them bills. They uncover hundreds, thousands maybe, of due bills. Captain Thibidoux, he ain't paid hard cash money for nothing all his adult life. Come to find out, he owe every shop in New Orleans. Not even one of them china chamber pots in the Royal Street townhouse belong to him outright."

He took a brooding sip of the oversweetened coffee.

"One stack of bills, that maybe tower a foot high, been weighed down with a silver bust of Napoleon. The captain always saying Napoleon his particular hero, but when they go to sell that silver bust along with every stick else, they discover it ain't even sterling but only

78

plate." Anger slanted across his eyes again. "Captain Alphonse Phillipe René Thibidoux always saying how much he admire Napoleon. But when the truth come out, the bust he got of that great man of his ain't even real silver. Ain't but a silver wash over cheap copper and lead."

3

"HOW COME THERE HAVEN'T been any battles? I thought there was supposed to be a war on." Saranell laid Madison in her lap and rested her back against the side of the barn to watch Renny work. "Papa's been gone a month now, and still nobody's fought anybody else."

"Ain't nobody but a fool itching to fight under this July sun." He was chopping a cedar stump that lay between the barn and the grove of balm-of-Gilead trees that gave the plantation its name, and he hefted the axe for another blow.

She frowned. "What about the Abolitionists? Don't they want a war?"

"Yeah, them maybe."

"And what about Lincoln? Doesn't he want a war? Isn't he ready to fight? Papa says he's not as empty-headed as he's made out to be in the papers."

"Likely nobody that stupid," Renny agreed without interest. He chopped again at the heart of the stump, laying open a gash of scarlet wood, before he leaned the axe against the barn and took up a shovel. He jabbed the blade into the ground next to the roots. "Ain't no use to saw down a juniper if you leave it to sprout again. If your mama want rose bushes here, then we got to kill off the whole thing."

"Why does Mama want roses by the barn?"

"Who got any idea why women want what they want?"

"I know why I want things."

"You ain't no woman. You just a little girl." He grinned at her. "When you grow up, you going to do what every other woman do, decide for something, forget what you decided, or if you remember, then you likely change your mind."

"I won't either."

"You wait and see." He emptied a shovelful of rock fragments from around the cedar root and drove the shovel back into the earth.

"Well, if you want to know what I think—" Saranell began.

The ring of iron against iron sang from the hole.

She and Renny stared at each other.

Then they fixed their eyes on the cedar stump as Renny withdrew the shovel and swung it into the dirt again. Again the shovel struck metal.

"Hey, maybe we got us some buried treasure here." He arched the blade into the ground close to the stump, and metal clanged. "Hoo—ee! This something bigger than a rusty nail caught in them roots."

Saranell jumped up, draped Madison over her arm, and hopped across the hot, stony topsoil. She stopped on a tuft of fescue to stand close to Renny. "Maybe it's pirate gold!"

"We too far from the sea for pirates. But maybe Doc Webster leave behind a box of cash money when he sell this place to your pa."

He dug again, and Saranell stared as an iron curve rose between two branches of the root. "Hoo—ee!" she echoed. "There's the handle of a treasure chest!"

"Hold on. But could be."

Two more blows of the shovel lifted a circle of iron.

"I can tell it's not a handle, but maybe it's the ring on top of the chest," she offered hopefully.

"Hold on," he said again.

The shovel blade brought up an object in the outline of an iron vase filled with hardened mud. Welded iron bands formed a globe topped by a wide iron rim.

"What is it?" She peered closer. "Some kind of metal cage?"

"No, look, them four iron bands too far apart for a cage. Anything you put in it get out lickity split."

"Why has it got a padlock on the rim then?"

"Just hold on."

He shook the dry mud clods loose. The iron bands formed a hollow vessel ten inches in diameter and a foot long. A disk the size of a biscuit had been welded to one band, and four thick, blunted nails, like the dulled tines of a huge fork, protruded in right angles from the interior of the disk.

"What is it?" Saranell repeated.

Renny upended it with the rim and padlock uppermost, and they studied it.

"Don't look like nothing," he said finally. "It sure ain't no treasure."

"Nope."

He tipped it over, and the broad band and lock became a pedestal.

"Now it's got the shape of a head," Saranell said. "With that wide rim and the padlock as a collar."

Abruptly Renny stiffened. His eyelids lowered over his eyes like brown leaves.

Saranell turned to watch him. "Do you know what it is?"

He raised his arm and slammed the metal shell against the ground. It rolled with an iron thud into the barn wall. "Piece of slave trash," he growled.

"What do slaves use it for?" she asked quickly, before he could stride away.

He glared at the sphere lying like an empty iron skull. His lips firmed as if he didn't intend to answer her, but after half a minute, he said, "Ain't slaves use it. Masters, overseers, they the ones who use it."

"What do they do with it?"

There was another long pause before he said in a tight voice, "They fit it over the head of a slave. Like a mask. To punish him."

"What do they punish him for?"

"Don't matter. Whatever they decide he might be doing. Or maybe done. Or might think of doing. Or maybe what they think he might consider doing sometime. They put them iron bands over his head with them prongs in his mouth, pressing his tongue so he can't swallow, and then they lock him in."

"Why shouldn't he swallow?"

"Ain't that he shouldn't. Just that he can't. A slave mask like that all very efficient, see. The overseer snap it on some field hand, and he still got his hands and feet free to go up and down the rows and hoe cotton out in the sun. Ain't nobody be wasting his back labor by loading him down with chains. Nobody be putting him in a cell so he don't work and maybe even get some rest. That ain't no punishment."

He gave her a grim look. "This way, with that mask on his head, they get the field work done. The slave out there working while still being punished. Them prongs keep him from swallowing, and if the summer sun beat down strong enough—" His plum colored eyes glittered. "—if it get hot enough to fry eggs on a rock, that iron heat up like a stove. At sundown when they lift off the mask, the nose skin peel away, all cooked and juicy like a slab of ham."

"Ugh!"

He swerved away from her and strode toward the slave cabins.

He didn't look back, and Saranell watched him disappear into the hut he shared with Ozra.

Then she approached the slave mask and crouched down to examine it. "Sometimes I think Renny makes things up," she said softly.

She poked at the iron mask, and it rocked. Sunlight caught a circle molded in the iron collar, and she peered closer.

"Look, Madison, here's a label."

The circle held an embossed tulip and letters still caked with mud. Saranell scratched the logo with a fingernail and angled the metal bands toward the sun to read, "Made in Boston."

She released the mask and stood up. She held Madison steady on her shoulder as she backed away.

"If that's the way they treat their slaves in the North—" she breathed, "no wonder Papa has to go fight the Yankees!"

4

"WELL, IF YOU'D RATHER wander around Fisk's store than spend the afternoon at Rosegate with me—" Geneva glanced at Saranell in the carriage seat beside her. "But I personally won't set foot in town until this war nonsense is over. You can't imagine how tiresome it is without a single presentable man in sight." She laughed. "But, of course, you can't imagine it, can you? You'll have to be older to care whether handsome men are present or not."

Saranell didn't smile. "A box of wooden legs and books is coming up the river, and I heard Mr. Fisk say that one of the books might be by Mr. Dickens."

"Fanny Culver is trying to put on a brave face now that Haze has gone off to England. Of course, none of us can mention it serves her right that he took Cassy with him." She sidled her gaze toward Saranell and laughed again. "But you'll have to be older to understand that, too, won't you?"

Saranell nearly said that she understood quite well, that she knew Mr. Culver had eloped with Mrs. Culver's maid, but Geneva went on before she said it. "Fanny's showing us all how calm and how uncon-cerned she is, so she's having her cook bake a marshmallow cake. It's terribly sweet for adults, but children usually like it. You'd probably enjoy it. And you could play at Rosegate with little Viola Culver."

Saranell frowned. "Viola Culver still sucks her thumb."

"Fanny was too old to have a baby, but she had to show Haze she was still capable of bearing children. That's the only reason he married her in the first place." Geneva stared at the mountains across the river.

Then she looked back at Saranell as Renny turned the horses into the Rosegate drive. "Well, do what you like. Go on to Fisk's if you want to." She gestured to Renny. "Pull close to the veranda. I have no intention of ruining these new slippers with yellow clay just because Fanny Culver is too cheap to buy a decent gardener."

"Yes'm."

The carriage swayed to a halt, and Renny jumped off the driver's box to hand Geneva down.

When he climbed onto the box again and gentled the horses forward, Saranell relaxed into the carriage cushions and watched the woods slide by.

After twenty minutes, the carriage passed mansions flanked by vast lawns and chestnut trees, then more modest townhouses surrounded by flower gardens and contained by fences, and finally the green of the college and the gray stones of the Episcopal Church. At last they reached the hot, silent square.

No one else was on the street.

Renny stopped the horses in the alley between Fisk's General Store and the closed stage office.

"I'll be right back." Saranell climbed down quickly, jogged around the corner, and entered the dark store whose only light came from the front window.

"Mr. Fisk gone home for his tea," a voice bellowed at once. A figure with the pale complexion of a cave fish and an overly large head waited beside the pyramids of tinned fruit at the far end of the store.

"Are you sure, Quincy Drood?"

"Yes'm, Miss Saranell." He bobbed his great round head and nodded a long time. "Noah carry him. A soldier come with letters, and Mr. Fisk, he go home to read his. Your mama got one, too, Miss Saranell."

"A letter? From Papa?"

"Yes'm, Miss Saranell." He disappeared below the counter and popped up again. "See!" he shouted with satisfied glee. He held out an envelope.

She took it, but the light was too dim to tell if he'd indeed given her a letter from her father.

"Mr. Fisk, he leave me in charge, and I can fetch what you come in for, Miss Saranell."

"I came for a book, but—"

"A reading book? I can reach down a book."

He bounded from behind the counter and scurried up a ladder closer to the front window. "I know where Mr. Fisk put them new books!"

He wobbled on the ladder a moment before he slid down the rungs again with four books cradled in one arm. He hopped to the floor and spread the books out neatly before Saranell. "See, I know where Mr. Fisk keep them new books."

Saranell peered down to read the titles and authors aloud. "*Mill on the Floss* by Mr. Eliot, *Origin of the Species* by Mr. Darwin, *Principles of Geology* by Mr. Lyell, *Great Expectations* by Mr. Dickens."

She scooped up the last. "This is the one I wanted."

Quincy Drood smacked his lips with delight. "Mr. Fisk put me in charge."

She looked at his eyes, as dull and flat as bottle corks, and weighed the book in her hands while she said, "Papa told me before he left that he'd buy me some new books to make up for Miss Sawyer not having school this year. His troop signed up for only ninety days, but somebody else might come in and buy this book before the end of the month. Maybe I better take it now."

"Yes'm, Miss Saranell."

She opened the leather cover, but since the light was still too dim to make out the print, she merely put the letter inside. "All right. I'll take it. Can you remember to tell Mr. Fisk that Papa will pay for it when he comes home?"

"I won't forget, Miss Saranell," he said obediently.

"And tell him that Papa will be home by the end of the month."

"Yes'm, Miss Saranell."

"All right. I'm going to take it with me. But don't forget to tell Mr. Fisk."

"I won't forget, Miss Saranell," he repeated, exactly as he'd said it before.

Then he swooped back to the counter, uncapped a glass jar to grab a wrapped taffy, and held it out proudly. "Mr. Fisk, he always give candy to good customers."

"I don't think—"

"Mr. Fisk, he leave me in charge."

She gazed at him a moment, then she took the candy. "Thank you."

She walked through the store and out into the sunlight, and even as she blinked to adjust her eyes against the glare, she reopened the book to look at the letter. There was no stamp, but she didn't expect one since her father refused to buy Union postage, and she sighed with relief at the simple address, "Geneva Birdsong, Balm-of-Gilead Plantation," while she said aloud, "It's Papa's handwriting all right."

When she rounded the corner and approached the waiting landau, Renny frowned. "What you got there?"

She climbed onto the driver's box beside him. "It's a book by Mr. Dickens and a letter from Papa."

"And that?"

She opened her palm to show the papered taffy. "What does it look like?"

"Where you get hard money for them things?"

"Papa said he was going to buy me some new books."

"And some new candy?"

"Quincy Drood was in charge of the store, and he said Mr. Fisk always gives good customers a treat."

Renny pointed his whip at the horses. "May as well leave Patches or Rosie here in charge as feeble Quincy." He gave Saranell a disapproving scowl. "You know better than that. Taking advantage of some simpleton like Quincy Drood."

"I didn't take advantage of him."

"A new book and candy for free ain't taking advantage?"

"Papa will pay for the book when he comes home. And Quncy Drood really wanted me to have the taffy. I'd have hurt his feelings if I'd refused it."

Renny eyed her another second before he shrugged. "Well, I guess you couldn't rightly hurt his feelings. But don't you take no more free candy. No telling what notions that big-headed fool get in his brain."

She unwound the paper and stretched the taffy apart. She pulled until the strand snapped in two, and then she held out half to Renny.

"You trying to bribe me?" But he removed his glove and took the candy.

Saranell held her piece gingerly. "Did I tell you there was a letter from Papa?"

"You know you did."

"Shall I read it to you?"

"Don't your mama want to see it first?"

"I don't think she cares. She doesn't like to hear about the war, so she gives me all the letters to keep after I read them to her." She put the taffy in her mouth and sucked on it for a moment. "It'll be another couple of hours before Mama's ready to leave Mrs. Culver's house. What if Papa wants something from town? It'd be a shame to come all the way back when we're here now."

"It'd be a real shame to wear out old Patches and Rosie here," he agreed sarcastically as he gentled the horses into a walk.

"And if it rains, then the carriage could get stuck in the mud."

"It ain't going to rain."

She rolled the chunk of taffy around in her mouth. Then she determinedly loosened the wax from the envelope. "You want to hear this or not?"

"How come I got a feeling you fixing to read it to me whether I do or not?"

She frowned at him and wedged the candy inside her cheek. "It's dated August 10, 1861." She began to read in a stilted voice, "*We have camped for the last two days near Oak Hills. Here our first clash of arms has taken place. We saw the enemy advancing and faced them, marching in a battle line. Balls fell thick as hail around us, and the enemy commenced firing shell and canister. One of the shots blew up Early Yarborough's sutler's wagon—*" She glanced at Renny, but he merely sucked on his own taffy. "*—so Early has become one of our troopers. After about thirty minutes we silenced the enemy guns and drove their infantry back to the stream. We won the day with the loss of only a captain, a lieutenant, two sergeants, and three privates.*"

There was no signature, and Saranell stopped reading.

"That's all." She looked at Renny, but when he didn't say anything, she pressed him with, "There's been a battle with the enemy, and Papa's troop won. That's good news, don't you think?"

He shifted the candy in his mouth. "Probably not for the captain, lieutenant, two sergeants, and three privates," he said.

5

THREE WEEKS LATER, without warning, the rainy season began.

Rain beat against the trees and bushes of Balm-of-Gilead Plantation, washed across the driveway and fields, swept pebbles through dead weeds and grass.

Saranell sat on the porch with Madison and *Great Expectations*.

"I wish the book had been longer," she said to the doll as she watched her mother's maid Tawny going toward Geneva's bedroom.

Tawny, very tall under her cloud of orange hair, could easily wear Geneva's old gowns after the lace had been clipped off and an apron added to make the hand-me-downs into slave wear. But since Geneva preferred gowns of crimson silk, the dresses did no more for Tawny's butterscotch skin and wild hair than they did for Geneva's pale complexion and wolfish yellow eyes.

Tawny rarely spoke, never met anyone's gaze, and now she floated into Geneva's bedroom and closed the door without a sound.

Saranell turned back to stare out at the wall of water beyond the veranda. "But I guess I can read the book again. I won't have to look up so many words, and maybe I won't even want Pip to marry Estella this time."

But she didn't move to open the leather cover and sat gazing at the rain.

She was still staring at the rushing water when the ghost of a horse suddenly appeared in the silver curtain.

No sound of hooves had reached the house through the tattoo of rain, but a sodden horse carrying a sodden rider had approached the house. The rider wore an officer's hat with a wide brim, and Saranell whispered with delicious horror, "It's a Yankee!"

Her hands tightened on Madison. "Papa said no Yankees would cross the Missouri border. But now one's here!"

The officer dismounted, tied his horse to a tree, lifted a saddlebag from the saddle, and sloshed across the lawn to the porch.

"The Yankees are here." Saranell's whisper became hoarse with excitement. "They've come to take charge of our plantation."

But the officer who broke through the sheet of rain was Ian Birdsong. "Papa!"

Saranell jumped up, dropped Madison and the book into the wicker seat of the rocker, and lunged against her father. "I thought you were a Yankee!"

Ian threw a wet arm around her and smiled. "I guess I ain't."

Out of the rain, he looked much the same as when he'd ridden away three months before. But anyone who knew Ian Birdsong well would see at once that something about him had changed.

It wasn't merely that he was thinner or that outdoor exercise had tanned his face. Or that his once-tight uniform now fit loosely. Or that he seemed unaware of the discomfort of a soaked uniform and boots. It was something in the fact that his smile failed to reach his eyes when he said, "Go find your mother, Saranell. Tell her I'm here for tea."

Saranell, who may or may not have noticed the change, ran into the hall. "Mama! Mama! Papa's here!" She knocked at Geneva's door. "Papa's home!"

Only silence came from the room.

"Mama!"

No one in the house ever knew if the mistress of the plantation would open the door of her bedroom or if she'd merely ignore anyone who knocked, and Saranell had raised her hand again when the door abruptly swung back and Tawny stood staring at some point beyond Saranell's auburn curls.

"Mama! I thought the Yankees had come, but it was Papa! Papa's here!" The words tumbled into Geneva's room, with its great tester bed and sugar chest that gave the walls an odor of candy, and Saranell added quickly before Tawny could shut her out, "He says he's come for tea."

Geneva lay on her bed wrapped in a crimson dressing gown. Her pale fingers entwined across her chest, and her bare feet, so white they appeared clad in pale stockings, jutted from beneath the hem of the gown. "Well, well, so your father has finally had his fill of soldiering."

A bony hand gestured toward Tawny. It was the hand on which she wore her multipearled engagement ring, and the pearls glowed with milky light. "Get my ribbons and slippers from the press." Her fingers completed an arch to include Saranell. "Go tell Zilla to steep some blackberry leaves and tell her to make a pastry."

Saranell nodded, raced off, and plunged into the rain between the house and kitchen. She stuck her head into the kitchen door and shouted Geneva's orders to the cook, but she didn't wait to hear Zilla complain as she sped back to the house and raced onto the porch again.

Ian Birdsong had sunk into a wicker chair, and he gave her his unfinished smile while she flicked water from her hair. "I wasn't a Yankee coming out of the rain this time. But remember, if the Yankees do get close, your mama promised to pack up and go to your Aunt Nora's in Tyler."

"I remember, Papa. But Mama said—"

Geneva had said she had no intention of fleeing either to Ian's boring sister or to any other small hick town in Texas, but Saranell swallowed before she repeated her mother's words about her aunt and Texas, and a silence fell.

It lasted until Ian glanced at the book in the chair and said, "I see you haven't forgotten how to read."

"No, Papa." She gazed at him kindly and wiped her wet face.

"Is this novel good?"

"I didn't much like the ending, but I'm going to read it again and see if it's better this time."

He nodded. "Sometimes you have to give an ending a second chance."

"I got the book at Fisk's store, and now that you're back—"

But before she could tell him about having taken the book on credit, Geneva's laugh chimed from the doorway. "Well, well, Ian Birdsong, so your ninety-day enlistment is up. It's about time you quit parading around in those prairie campsites and marching through towns to impress young ladies with your splendid uniform. It's about time you came back to the plantation."

Ian Birdsong sprang to his feet and she extended a white hand to him. But a stranger coming upon the scene couldn't have guessed from her cool reception that the colonel on her porch was more than a passing acquaintance.

"I wouldn't have been able to keep this place together much longer, waiting for you to come home," she said. "We're out of everything. And there's nothing in town to buy. The tea we have to make do with is dried blackberry leaves, there's not a speck of cinnamon left for pies, and we've started on the final cone of sugar."

She picked up her scarlet hem and wove toward a wicker chair, avoiding the pools of water her husband had left on the porch. "Sometimes I think it makes sense to do what Haze Culver did and go to Europe," she added coldly. "And it's about time you were mustered out of that ridiculous army."

"I ain't home for good quite yet." He sat down near her, but not close enough to drip rainwater on her dressing gown. "The enlistment of the troop was up all right, but—"

Geneva interrupted irritably, "Well, if the enlistment period was up, then of course, you're back."

He glanced down, back up at her shyly. "General McCulloch wrote to Jeff Davis that he could let the Missouri men go home, but he insisted he couldn't do without the Arkansas soldiers. President Davis himself urged us to rejoin."

He looked at Saranell and smiled. "So the whole troop reenlisted for the duration of the war. Even if it takes until Christmas to defeat the Yankees—which no one believes it will, of course—the Arkansas Fourteenth is going to stay with the army."

6

CHRISTMAS NEARED, but Ian Birdsong didn't return.

Instead, snow replaced the rain, and a Confederate company from New Orleans, the Pelican Rifles, arrived to camp on the college lawn in the center of town.

"Fanny Culver is going to throw a holiday ball for all those charming Louisiana boys," Geneva said to Saranell from her bed. She coughed. "At least there are men in Fayetteville again."

Saranell had brought her a cup of sassafras tea, and she accepted it with a wrinkle of her nose. "Since I have this wretched cold, and since your father's the one who enjoys holidays and he's nowhere in sight, I'm not going to wear myself out with Christmas this year." She put the teacup on the sugar chest that served as her night table and her pale hand shooed Saranell into the hall. "Go make those paper flowers of yours and have one of the servants bring in a tree if you want, but I've got to save what little strength I have."

So that same afternoon Saranell tramped through the snow, looking at trees with Renny.

"That one got the proper height," he said toward a tall cedar. "And it got a nice green color to it."

"It's funny shaped."

Renny sighed and broke another path through the snow.

He stopped before another tree. "This one got the most branches we seen yet."

"Look at that bare spot in the back."

"All cedars got a bare spot some place."

"It looks scraggly to me."

"All cedars look scraggly, too," he said. "That kind of tree the most scraggly in creation. That the reason why they decide to use cedars for Christmas trees. Christmas the season you got to forgive things, so you get in some good forgiving practice by starting with your puny tree."

"Aw-w-w."

He grinned at her.

She moved on a few steps. "Let's look at one of those over there."

He followed her. "Well, that one don't seem no more spindle-shanked than the rest we been studying. I could make do with it. We best pick one soon anyway since any minute now, them hummock clouds across the river fixing to dump another foot of snow on us."

She nearly asked him how he knew so many words, but since he might have been right about the snow, she glanced around quickly. "How about that one?"

He sighed again. "What you bet when I get it chopped down, you discover all them sorry looking branches? Remember, I ain't cutting but one."

"I think it looks good. And I can make lots of paper flowers."

"Any one we see so far got to have at least two bushel of them paper flowers."

He gauged the fall line. "You back off now so them top branches don't crack you on the head when the trunk break loose."

She did as he ordered and stood on one cold foot and then the other as he chopped.

When the tree crashed into the snow it was obvious that it was indeed as scruffy as any they'd seen. She couldn't admit that he'd been right, however, so she followed him silently into the house and watched him set the tree on a cross of wooden lath in the parlor.

"But I should have had him put the tree up in the kitchen," she said to Madison half an hour later as she crouched near the sparse branches.

The doll bent forward, her glass curls nearly tipping her red cotton boots, surrounded by yarn and the blue paper wrappers from sugar cones, wrappers Saranell saved all year to make her Christmas flowers.

A single candle flame burned on the hearth and, since there was no fire in the fireplace, Saranell's hands in the candlelight appeared as blue as the paper. Her teeth clacked as she worked with cold scissors and an icy dinner knife. "What good is it to have servants if you can't even get somebody to build you a fire in the parlor when you want one?" Her hands shook as she sliced another paper row with the scissor blades and curled the slits with the dull edge of the knife. "When I grow up, I'm going to have my slaves build a fire in every fireplace in my house all winter long."

Her cold fingers faltered through the scraps of yarn, finally selected a purple strand and knotted it around the blue sugar paper.

When she held it by the knotted stem, the paper ruffles blossomed into a mock blue flower.

"I don't care how many stupid junipers or balm-of-Gilead trees Renny has to cut down, I'm going to keep my parlor as warm as the kitchen."

She took up another length of yarn, this one butternut gray, and tied the blue flower to the nearest cedar branch.

She rested sadly on her heels to watch the curled blue petals bob in the candlelight.

"It's no fun without Papa here to appreciate the results."

She laid the scissors and knife down among the scattered papers as Geneva appeared in the doorway.

"I can't stay in this dull house another minute. And I refuse to miss one more holiday party." She coughed and scowled, as if she expected an argument, while she twisted the pearl ring on her finger. "I heard that Fanny is having an afternoon tea for the soldiers, and I intend to go and have a splendid time."

She tensed for another cough. "Go tell Renny to harness the horses and tell him to wrap some warmed bricks in flannel to put under the lap robes."

Saranell hopped up, not admitting to Geneva or to herself that she was relieved to be sent on an errand to the kitchen where it was warm, and scooped up Madison.

She wore slave brogans around the plantation during the winter, and in the heavy awkward shoes, she fluffed happily through the snow on the brick pathway and reached the kitchen. "Renny!"

But no one sat before the great fireplace where an oak fire blazed, and she glanced around. "Renny!"

When nothing stirred, she laid the doll in a rocking chair and went back outside. She jumped from footprint to footprint in the set of snow tracks leading to the barn. "Renny!"

The barn was warm with animal breath and bodies, and a pale gold light sifted from the loft. Renny stood straddling Patches's hind hoof while he dug at the horse's iron shoe with a pick.

He and the horse looked up as Saranell burst in.

Patches and Rosie whinnied happily, and the little mule Toby threw himself against his stall with delight.

"Renny! Nobody's in the kitchen. Where is everybody? Where's Zilla?"

"How come I been delegated everybody's keeper around here?" He worked the pick. But just as Saranell had decided he wasn't going to volunteer anything else, he went on, "Zilla down sick at her cabin like usual when there snow on the ground. Nancy sneak off to visit her cousin over to Pate's, Tawny be hiding somewhere warm I wager, and old Ozra napping hard as he can. So how come you been shouting out there like the house fixing to collapse?"

"Mama's going to a tea party at Rosegate. She wants you to get the carriage ready."

"Your mama ain't well enough around that cold to be in a carriage in this wet snow."

"She says the outing will do her good. She wants some hot bricks in flannel under the carriage robes."

"Hot bricks ain't about to keep warm all the way to Rosegate."

A pebble bounced from the rim of the horseshoe onto the hay-strewn floor.

"But ice and snow and cool-down bricks don't mean no never-mind to a woman when she decide to go out." He lowered the hoof to the ground and patted the bay's flank. "You good as new now, Patches, so don't you be faking no pitiful hobble. I ain't falling for no sorry limp again."

Patches neighed. Toby lunged the stall door again and gave a high-pitched whinny.

"You dead right about that," Renny said.

"What did they say?" Saranell stuck a hand through the slats to fondle Toby's ears.

"They say they ain't hankering to be out in this marrow-cracking cold. And they add that if Saranell Birdsong got one particle left of the sense she born with, she best scoot inside to warm up by the kitchen fire."

"They did not."

But she nonetheless kissed Patches on the nose, stroked Rosie's neck, and padded across the hay carpet and back through the snow to the kitchen.

She dragged the rocker near the fire and sat down with Madison on her lap to study the flames. And when Renny, dressed in his red livery, came in a few minutes later to place half a dozen bricks by the grate, she looked at him sleepily. "Is it going to snow again?"

"In all likelihood."

He revolved the bricks as if he were toasting loaves. "But like I say, that don't mean no never-mind when a woman determined to do something she got a hankering to do."

As soon as he added more logs to the fire, replaced the fire screen, and bundled the hot bricks in flannel, he went out and shut the kitchen door.

The snap of the burning wood lulled the afternoon. The snow-light waned in the window and blew snow from the roof past the glass.

Saranell sank into herself before the glow of the fire.

She was jolted by a sudden hand on her shoulder. "Your mama send me to fetch you."

7

RENNY SHOOK her lightly.

She glanced around. She still sat in the kitchen, but the afternoon light seemed the same as when she'd settled into the rocking chair. She struggled to wake up and slid her feet into the slave brogans she'd kicked off to warm her toes. "How come you didn't go to Rosegate?"

He didn't answer but went back to the kitchen door and opened it for her. "Come on now."

New snow had fallen, and the drifts between the kitchen and the back door lay beneath a sugary crust that snapped with her every step.

She stamped off the snow as she went down the hall to her mother's room.

"Would anyone believe I trekked all the way to Rosegate through this ridiculous snow only to discover that the tea had been canceled and that Fanny Culver is packing to leave town before the Yankees arrive?"

"Are the Yankees coming?"

"Who knows? The Louisiana boys think so. And Fanny's convinced." She threw open the door to her armoire. "Well, if she can go, so can we."

She glanced around the room with disdain. "Your father's been urging us to go if the Yankees get close, and since now perhaps they're coming—" Her laugh tangled in her cough. "We'll just leave."

She began pulling out dresses and dropping them on the bed. "Well, Ian Birdsong, this trip is going to cost you. I'm going to need trunks of new things."

"Are we going to Aunt Nora's?"

"No, we are certainly not going to your Aunt Nora's. Or to deadly dull Tyler, Texas. We're going to Arkadelphia or Washington where the generals have set up headquarters, and where all the interesting balls are going to be."

Saranell shook her head with awe as her mother flung out the last of her gowns, closed the mirrored door, and circled the room.

"How will Papa know where we are?"

"You can write to him as soon as we decide where we're going."

She threw a red velvet cape lined with fur on the coverlet. "I'm giving that to Tawny. She may as well get some good out of it. I think the lining's made of cat. I sneeze every time I wear it."

Her lemon-pulp eyes skimmed across the pile of clothes on the bed to Saranell. "Now go bundle up two of everything you own—stockings, dresses, petticoats, everything you'll need—and put them in that carpetbag of your father's. But no books. We don't have room for books. Go tell Renny to pack the sterling in meal bags and put them on the floor of the carriage. I refuse to serve the generals even thistle tea without a decent silver set. And then go locate Tawny to come help me pack."

Saranell stood only a few seconds before she dashed back through the hall to the kitchen. "Zilla! Renny! Mama says the Yankees are coming!"

Again no one was there, and she whirled and ran to the barn. "Renny!"

Patches and Rosie still remained in the carriage shafts from the drive to Rosegate, and Renny was fitting a bit and harness onto Toby.

"Renny! We're leaving Gilead."

"So I been hearing all the way back from Rosegate Plantation. But Arkadelphia nor Washington ain't no place to be going with all them other refugee families pouring in and hoarding up what they afraid somebody else get to first."

She watched him. "Have you already packed Mama's silver?"

"It look like to you I got bags of silver on that buggy floor?" He gave her a disgusted glance. "You ever calculate how much sterling them cupboards hold?"

"Do you think the Yankees are really coming?"

He shrugged. "The grapevine have it them Louisiana soldiers see a parcel of Yankees coming whether anyone else do or not. They aim to empty out the grain and hay they can't carry off so the Yankees won't get no good out of what they leave. I hear them bayou boys fixing to burn down some buildings as well."

"Why would they do that?"

He shrugged again. "Keep the Yankees camping out in the snow, I guess. The military mind ain't extra logical that I can see."

She frowned. "Papa's in the military."

He didn't respond but continued to buckle a cinch around Toby as if she'd already gone. She was forced to walk stiffly away.

Just beyond the barn door, however, she broke into a run, racing to the slave quarters to alert the servants that they'd all be leaving.

She shouted into each doorway, "We're leaving Gilead! Everybody get ready! The Yankees are coming and we're leaving."

At Tawny's and Nancy's cabin, she added excitedly, "Come quick, Tawny. Mama needs you to help her pack.

She didn't try to explain as she raced back to the house to get her father's carpetbag, which she carried to her own room. As she opened it beside her bed, she murmured, "Everything's going so fast."

She started bundling jumpers, petticoats, and pantaloons into the bag.

Then she dropped prone to the hooked rug and stretched out on her stomach to look under the bed. She found a pair of white satin slippers and dragged them out, trailing a dust ball. She sat up to touch their little mother-of-pearl buttons before she tossed them back under the bed.

"Even Mama knows slave brogans are more practical for the snow," she said.

An hour later, she shoved the loaded carpetbag into the hallway, laid Madison across the handles and wrapped herself in the gray cloak her mother had ordered made from the leftover material from her father's uniforms.

Then she clattered in the slave shoes down the hall to her mother's room.

Geneva was tying the red velvet ribbons on her fur-lined bonnet and saying to Tawny, "Put my jewelry in that leather case and bring my gloves over here. I'll wear my pearl ring on the outside of the glove."

Geneva had always poked fun at Ian's pearl engagement ring, laughing as she held it out for exhibition. "The pearls look like soap bubbles frothing from a bottle, don't they?" But she wore the ring constantly, and she seemed to value its extravagance even as she always laughed when she added to her listeners, "The foolish man. He rode straight up to my papa's veranda and dropped the ring in my lap and asked me to marry him. He'd only met me once."

And as she now smoothed the gloves on her long bony fingers, she slid the ring over the soft leather.

But for once, she didn't laugh.

"Well, Ian Birdsong, you kept insisting we leave. And so now we are." She gazed around her bedroom. "But did you think what I was supposed to do with the heirloom chairs and the paintings? And did you imagine how I would be able to pack the crystal apple Haze gave me for my sixteenth birthday?"

Then she glanced quickly at Saranell. "Did you get everything you need? And did you leave all your books behind?"

Saranell nodded for both questions. "But how are we going to get all the servants in the carriage, Mama?"

Geneva circled her arm with a sable muff, whose fur matched her bonnet rim, while she coughed. "I suppose it's too much to ask that the Yankees wait until warmer weather. What did you say?"

"How can all the servants fit in the carriage? Especially with all the bags of silver on the floor."

"All the servants aren't going in the carriage. There isn't room in the landau for seven."

"I don't think they can all walk behind, Mama. Old Ozra can't keep up with Patches and Rosie. Nancy's had a bad leg since she got it caught in the hay binder that time, and Zilla's awfully fat to be—"

"They aren't going."

"But I told them—"

"Don't worry about them. I need Tawny, and we must have a driver, so they're going with us, but the other servants will be perfectly fine right where they are. The Yankees may pass through the countryside, but they won't stay." She tucked at her vermilion riding coat. "This war is too ridiculous to last much longer. The whole thing's bound to be over by summer. We'll be back by then, so the servants may as well stay here and look after the place."

Saranell stared at her in stunned silence. "But, Mama, will there be enough food and wood to last through the winter? Zilla says the cellar's almost empty already."

"Zilla always exaggerates. If the Yankees do ride by here, she can ask them for food. The Union Abolitionists are the ones disrupting our lives, so they may as well take some responsibility and have their soldiers pass out bags of flour."

She swept from the room and strode down the hall.

Outside in the snow she looked at the little mule tied to the back of the carriage and her lips tightened. But she didn't say anything about him or about the other plantation servants who were straggling from their cabins. She merely held out her glove with the pearl ring for Renny to hand her into the landau.

"We'll stop in Fayetteville tonight."

As she settled herself on the cushions and put her feet on the lumpy sacks of silver, she looked over one shoulder toward Saranell. "If the servants keep on doing what they've been doing—whatever that is—I'm sure the Yankees won't harm them." She gestured to Tawny, who now wore the fur-lined cape over her faded dress and apron, and Tawny climbed onto the driver's box. She clasped the red cloak grandly around her hips as she sat down.

Renny lifted Saranell into the coach, and the hard edges of silver bowls pressed against her legs. Renny covered Geneva with the lap robes, tucked a quilt around Saranell, and handed her Madison before he lifted himself gracefully onto the driver's box beside Tawny.

"Haw!"

As the bays jerked the landau into motion, Saranell looked back.

The other servants lugged baskets and bundles and looked heavy and slow as they came from the quarters. They'd obviously layered on every piece of clothing they owned for the trip, and as they struggled through the snow they didn't seem yet to have noticed the carriage pulling away.

Suddenly snow began to drift from the sky and drop over the servants. The lazy, spiraling flakes blurred their outlines.

"We didn't tell anyone goodbye, Mama."

But Geneva didn't turn to glance at her slaves or her house as the carriage rolled down the driveway. She looked instead at the rows of winter-bare balm-of-Gilead poplars and said, "Well, if the Yankees are good for anything, maybe they'll chop down those dreadful trees for firewood."

8

THE CARRIAGE ROUNDED the curve.

The snow thickened, and after a few minutes the carriage forded the river. Saranell burrowed into the quilt, holding tight to Madison as ice flakes pocked her forehead.

She told herself two more times that the servants would be all right until summer when they'd be back.

Although she couldn't track the sun in the already cloudy sky, she was sure at least an hour had elapsed before the landau reached Rosegate.

The bays had nearly passed the entrance when Geneva called out suddenly, "Wait! It's too cold to be out with evening coming on. We'll just surprise Fanny and stop here for the night."

Renny headed the horses at once into the lane, and within seconds, the white columns of the house came into view through the snow.

But the house sat strangely quiet, and no smoke was visible curling from the chimneys.

Renny pulled up to the porch to hand Geneva down.

"How like Fanny to let even the kitchen fire go out completely," Geneva muttered quietly. "She was always the cheapest—"

She climbed the veranda steps and rapped on the door as she raised her voice and called out cheerfully, "Fanny, dear! We've decided to go with you to the south. We'll make a caravan."

The door remained shut, and the house stayed silent.

Geneva knocked once more, but almost immediately she pressed the door latch.

"Fanny!" She stepped inside. "Fanny! We've come to spend the night. We can all start for Fort Smith tomorrow!"

Renny bundled Saranell from the carriage and set her on the porch. She followed her mother into the cold hall.

Geneva had stopped at the door to the first parlor and was staring at the furniture covered by white sheets. The carpets had been rolled, and every piece of bric-a-brac had disappeared from the mantel and the shrouded tabletops.

"Who would believe Fanny Culver could get organized that fast," she said as she swept down the hall.

Saranell trailed after her to Fanny Culver's bedroom, where only rope netting now hung between the bed railings below carved bedposts.

Geneva surveyed the room with distaste. "Just as I thought."

Tawny came from the back hallway. "Ain't nobody here," she said, not looking at anyone.

"Well, that will make it easy for us to be guests, won't it?" Geneva turned from the stripped bed. "Hurry up and build a fire in this wretched little fireplace, and then dig out something to eat."

Tawny stood a moment in her flaring orange hair and scarlet cape, gazing toward the angle of wall and ceiling, before she said, "Ain't no food. The kitchen been picked clean. Ain't no wood neither."

Geneva burst into a laugh. "How like Fanny. To plan this trip for months, and then wait until the last minute to tell me. She might not even have mentioned it at all if I hadn't come by. She never could forgive me for the fact that Haze and I—" She broke off, untied her bonnet, and dropped it on the sheet-covered washstand. "Well, find what you can. And bring in the quilts from the carriage so I can lie down."

Tawny floated away, and Saranell followed her from the room.

She and Madison stood alone in the icy hallway a moment before she sighed and climbed the stairs to the second and then the third floor.

Rosegate's main house was twice the size of the Balm-of-Gilead Plantation house, and the top floor had been designed as a library rotunda with a stained-glass dome and wall-to-ceiling bookshelves.

But as Saranell reached the third floor, it was obvious that the Culvers had given up illusions of grandeur. The rotunda, bathed in a blue and roseate haze from the colored-glass design, had been turned into a child's playroom.

Scores of toys cluttered the floor, child-sized sofas and ottomans sat around the walls, a table and chair set—equipped with child-sized dishes and candelabra—stood beside a bent-wood rocking horse with a wooden head that resembled Patches, and the two bottom shelves of every bookcase were crammed with playthings made of wood, metal, and pottery.

A large doll house, a replica of Rosegate itself, complete with rotunda and furnished with miniature furniture and tiny dolls, dominated the center of the room.

"Look at all the toys, Madison," Saranell whispered. "It's like a shop."

She circled the room, looking at the blocks, the boxes of marbles and tops and tin animals, the jumbled nine-pins, balls, and iron banks cast into the shapes of clowns, cottages, and elephants. If the temperature hadn't been near freezing, she might have sat and poured tea for Madison at the little table, but since she continued to shudder with the cold even as she admired the various items, she at last clumped downstairs.

Renny had built a fire in Fanny Culver's bedroom and had stacked a pile of broken winter branches beside the bedroom hearth.

"Go into the parlor," Geneva ordered from Fanny Culver's four-poster bed as soon as Saranell appeared. "The servants have saved some cornbread for you." She turned toward the wall and coughed. "And shut that door so what warmth there is won't escape."

Saranell closed the door and hurried to the parlor, where another small fire burned, and where Tawny and Renny sat before it in chairs still covered with sheets.

"I wondered where you got to." Renny held out a kerchief of cornbread, and Saranell took it, climbed onto a chair, and drew a quilt around her.

As she ate, she said, "Will we be able to buy food in Washington if Mama decides to go there? You said people would be hoarding food."

He glanced at her. "Them refugees that reached there some time ago likely be hoarding up food all right. But since you ain't been pining for no caviar anyway, they probably got plenty of regular meal and beans. Them generals in charge down there ain't likely to skip morning biscuits even if they be out waging war."

She picked crumbs from the quilt. "That was a pretty little piece of cornbread. I'm still hungry."

"I expect we all still hungry," Renny said. "Don't be thinking on it. You think about your emptiness and it stretch bigger and bigger."

She brushed away yellow bits too small to taste. "You ought to see the toys they've got upstairs. I bet Viola Culver had every kind of toy you ever heard of."

Renny was silent a minute, but finally he said, "Haze Culver got cotton land down around Helena, and he suppose to be one rich white man." He gazed around the room. "Maybe he buy his little girl whatever she want—for show anyway—but he sure enough one stingy miser. They ain't nothing in his pantry, nor even salt on his smoke-house floor."

"Mama says Mrs. Culver is the cheap one."

"Wealthy white women usually do they husband's bidding. And with nothing atall here—" He held his palms toward the fire. "You get to wondering if this room ever been warm. I wager Ex-Major Haze Culver know long before he run away to England that he ain't coming back."

"Well, in that case—" Geneva stood in the parlor doorway, and the three of them started. "Since Haze didn't care a whit what Fanny—or anyone else—thought about his running away with Cassy, I don't think he can complain if we use his furniture to build up our fires."

Renny stared at her astounded. "Chop up the furniture!"

"You can start with the dining room set." Her hand, with the pearl ring still affixed over her kid glove, swung around the living room. "Or you can start in here with those end tables Fanny picked out herself in Philadelphia the Christmas before the war started. They're as tacky as everything else she ever chose except Haze."

9

GENEVA HAD ORDERED THEM all to be ready to leave Rosegate the following morning, but overnight, the snow and sleet became a blizzard, and the next day, drifts buried not only the driveway but the paths to the kitchen and outbuildings.

Renny had reluctantly broken up the living room end tables and the dining room chairs, but even with small fires in only two rooms, he'd been forced to start on the table and sideboard.

"Maybe your mama know pieces better than most peoples, but this look like solid mahogany to me," he grumbled while he unscrewed the table legs and prepared to chop them in two.

Saranell refused to discuss Rosegate furniture. "You ought to see the toys upstairs," she said as she tucked a quilt around Madison.

"How come you all of a sudden interested in playthings? You been keeping that china-headed doll because you ain't got friends close, but I thought you quit baby toys when you learned to read."

She scowled at him.

But when he didn't seem to notice her frown, she sighed and said, "There's the tiniest house. It's just like Rosegate, and it has tiny furniture and little people to go with it. You ought to see it."

"Nothing but play trash."

But after another hour of making firewood from the Culver's polished banquet table and mahogany buffet, he followed Saranell to the third floor to see the doll house.

They hunkered down beside it.

"See. What did I tell you?"

"My, my, look at that." He picked up a tiny blue velvet sofa and turned it over in his hands. "Just like a Lilliputian house."

"Like a what?"

He didn't answer as he got to his feet. "This room ain't got a fireplace. It some stupid to have a room you can't heat up on a snow day." He glanced around with disgust. "Go on to the parlor now while I fetch this house down."

Saranell clambered down the stairs to where Tawny sat before the fire, and Renny followed, balancing the miniature Rosegate.

He unrolled a carpet and set the doll house on it near the fireplace.

"But don't you be asking me to cart down nothing else," he said. "I got better things to be doing than to move toys around in them cold rooms."

Tawny turned her gaze slowly to the doll house.

As Saranell began to straighten the tumbled furniture, Tawny took up a tiny cradle with its tiny baby and held it gently in her palm.

For the first time since she'd been purchased by Ian Birdsong, Tawny's sand-colored eyes showed a spark of interest. But she didn't speak or look at Saranell beside her, and by the time Renny returned to the parlor with a stack of splintered drawers from the breakfront, she'd put aside the little cradle and doll and was gazing again into the flames.

The blizzard raged for two days.

When it finally ended, the plank table and benches from the kitchen, and most of the walnut pieces from three bedrooms, had been burned.

On the third day, the sun appeared, and ice diamonds sparkled in the drifts. The wind slacked, and the day dawned warm enough for Saranell to escape the smoky parlor in her gray cape.

"Hoo—ee." She grinned at Renny as she stopped by the well and watched him break through the snow toward the stable. "You can almost breathe out here."

"Almost."

She looked across the lawn toward the white slope down to the river. Then she stooped to ladle up a handful of snow. She tilted it back and forth to watch it glitter in the sunlight before she leaned into her hand to lick the crystals.

"Snow's so pretty, it should taste good," she said. "But it doesn't have any flavor at all."

"If we had us some molasses, we could pour it over a dish of snow and have us some fine tasting ice. If Mrs. Fanny Culver had left us a dish and a spoon, that is."

"Since we don't have a dish or any long sweetener, why not wish for maple syrup?" she asked peevishly. "I like it better."

"You getting downright crotchety in your old age. But maple syrup be all right with me." He ploughed through the drift. "Or maybe some brandy syrup like they got in New Orleans. Where they ain't got snow to pour it on."

He kicked the shed door free from the ice and tugged it open.

Neighs of welcome came from Patches, Rosie, and Toby.

"You all been chafing to get some air, ain't you?" Renny went inside.

"If the Louisiana troops did burn down some buildings, I bet the ruins look better covered with snow." She raised her voice so he could hear from inside the shed. Then she packed a snowball. "But we don't even know for sure if the town is burned. Or if Yankees are anywhere in sight."

She dropped the handful of snow as Renny came out and frowned toward the river.

"I said we still don't know if a single Yankee is anywhere close," she repeated.

He was staring down the slope. "Well," he said, "I guess we do now."

10

SARANELL whirled around.

Three horsemen were riding up the hill toward the house.

The one in the lead wore an officer's floppy brown hat and a thick blue overcoat. The other men sat in their saddles wearing homespun and jeans, but their blue caps and good boots readily identified them as Yankees.

They rode confidently, but when they got close, they slowed their horses and gazed from the kitchen to the spring house to the shed and slave quarters as if they'd never seen a plantation before.

The lead rider pulled up beside the smokehouse, and Saranell stared, openly hostile, at him.

The silence lengthened until Renny finally said, "Yes, sir? You be needing something?"

The man jerked as if he hadn't expected anyone to speak, or at least to speak in any language he could understand, and he studied Renny a long time before he said, "Who owns this place?"

"Marse Haze Culver own it. But the Birdsong family visiting here right now. They been caught in the snow storm."

The man, who had pale gray eyes in a tanned face, stared for another long moment before he asked, "Who owns you?"

Renny's eyelids flattened. He ignored the question and nodded toward Saranell. "That the Birdsong child."

The officer didn't repeat his question and looked at Saranell. "Your mama here with you, missy?"

Saranell lifted her chin disdainfully.

Renny said quickly, "Miss Geneva resting inside. She ain't well."

The Yankee officer remained silent as if he were having to translate what Renny said. Then his silvery eyes blinked toward Saranell. "You tell you ma we come by, missy, not meaning any mischief."

When she still didn't answer, he made a vague gesture with his leather glove. "We got strict orders to pay for what we get from you people. If you have horses, we need them, but we aim to buy them." He looked back at Renny. "You got any horses here?"

"They a couple in the shed."

"We ain't stealing. Understand that we ain't taking your stock without pay." He looked from Renny to Saranell. "We're offering twenty U.S. greenbacks for every horse, missy, which seems to me a fair price.

Ian Birdsong had paid three hundred dollars each for the matching bays, but Saranell didn't deign to say that.

The officer made another nervous gesture toward the two enlisted men sitting on their saddles in their homespun. "Go round up the horses."

They immediately climbed down.

One wore a gray undershirt under a greasy vest, but the other man had on a shirt of faded red plaid. They both wore cavalry boots, and they tramped down the snow as they went into the shed.

Welcoming neighs went up again while Tawny came from the back door wearing Geneva's red cloak and carrying one of Geneva's silver serving bowls full of water.

The silver rim reflected tiny suns, Tawny's orange hair flashed, and the taffeta of her dress shimmered. She didn't glance at Saranell or Renny or the Yankees as she flung out the water. It was as if she were alone in the yard of Balm-of-Gilead Plantation.

The crystal drops drilled instant holes in the snow.

The young soldier in the plaid shirt led Patches into the sunlight. He stumbled in the drifts while he stared open-mouthed at Tawny.

The other man came out leading Toby. "This here mule's got sores tolerable bad." He yanked the little mule toward the officer. He scratched at his gray shirt as he, too, gaped at Tawny.

The officer glanced at Toby's back.

From where Saranell stood, bloodied blotches along the bones of his spine were visible.

"He won't last long hauling with them sores." The scratching trooper spat a mouthful of brown tobacco saliva into the snow.

Renny had moved aside when they'd gone in the shed, and now he watched them from where he leaned against the fence.

"All right. Leave that one." The officer pointed at Renny. "Take him back inside."

"Yes, sir."

The man with the gray undershirt and the brown tobacco said disgustedly, "No wonder them Rebs ain't no match for our cavalry. The way they threat their horses and mules—"

Saranell stiffened with anger as the Yankee relinquished Toby's lead to Renny and returned to the shed for Rosie.

Tawny dried the silver bowl with a bit of toweling while the plaid-shirted man sauntered to where she was brushing snow off the well ledge to drape the wet rag.

"You a—a slave?" he asked.

The flaring orange hair raised as Tawny lifted her chin, but Saranell couldn't tell if she actually looked at the Yankee or at a spot in the sky.

"I'm from Kansas," the young soldier said. "My pa rode with John Brown." He had a very deep voice.

"All right, Seth. We're through here." The officer dismounted and plunged through the drifts toward Saranell. "You tell you ma now that we ain't meaning any mischief."

The young man continued to speak in a low voice to Tawny, but Saranell couldn't hear what he said as the officer repeated, "We're paying for them horses with good American dollars."

He held out some crumpled bills, but when Saranell made no move to take them, he anchored them under the silver bowl on the well.

"—if you want to come ride with us," the young man was concluding to Tawny.

Tawny finished smoothing the strip of toweling over the well rim. Then she turned, picked up the hem of Geneva's fur-lined cloak, and moved across the snow toward the Yankees.

The young man caught up to her with a skipping step.

When they reached the waiting horses, Tawny stopped beside Rosie and held her skirt and cape while she waited for the Yankee to make a hand stirrup for her.

He bent down and cupped his palms.

Tawny placed her shoe in them and lifted herself onto Rosie's back.

She settled and smoothed red velvet wings of the cloak across her lap with a lady-like hand.

Renny lounged half inside the shed while the Yankees climbed into their saddles.

The officer tied Patches's lead to his saddle horn. "Tell you ma that we paid a fair price," he repeated stubbornly.

Tawny gave a silent shake to Rosie's bridle, and she and the Yankee soldiers circled toward the river.

Saranell moved to stand beside Renny, who came from the shed to watch them.

The four riders and five horses became smaller and smaller as they moved down the snowy slope. The red worsted shirt and the red velvet cape glowed in the sunlight.

No one looked back.

"At least they left us Toby," Saranell said.

Renny nodded.

"But that Yankee said Toby had sores and was going to die."

Renny snorted. "Them Yankees don't know beans about horse flesh. Toby ain't never had a sore in his life. He the healthiest mule I ever see."

"But the Yankee said—"

"Them fellows ain't acquainted with horse hide nor with disease. No wonder the Yankees been having trouble winning. They send out soldiers too ignorant to be gathering stock. Knife scrapings ain't a bit like sores."

She stared at him. "You scraped Toby's back?"

"Not very deep. Just enough so he look like he got the mange. He don't even feel it."

She continued to stare. "How did you know they were coming?"

"Everybody know they going to be coming some time. Even if they ain't been in town yet like them Louisiana boys think, everybody know they going to be by one of these days."

He closed the door to the shed.

"I see them from the window splashing through the river water and starting up that slope." He fastened the hinge with a forked stick and shook his head. "But I sure wish I be able to shave old Rosie as well as Toby."

11

THE SNOW MELTED, but Geneva remained in Fanny Culver's bed-room without saying a word about the fact that a Yankee patrol had taken Tawny and the matched bays, without insisting that they set out with Toby for Fort Smith.

While Geneva lay in bed and Saranell sat on the parlor carpet and rearranged the doll furniture in the little house, Renny passed out the last cubes of cornbread and used up the store of dried apples and soft potatoes he'd brought from Balm-of-Gilead.

"Them bayou boys do a bang-up job on the town all right," he said the afternoon he returned from a walk into Fayetteville. "They burn down just about everything in sight. Nothing but rubble all the way to the square."

"They burned the college?"

"And that big church with them stain-glass windows."

She shook her head and put a tiny iron skillet on the miniature kitchen table. "Did you find any food?"

"Pate's Joseph tell me them boys pour out every barrel of flour in the storehouses before they grind the hay underfoot as they march out to meet them Yankees that ain't there. But along with no Yankees, they ain't one basket of corn in town neither. They hardly any stores and no buildings left in the square."

"Not even Mr. Fisk's store?"

Renny shook his head. "Up in smoke. But Joseph say Mr. Fisk pack up and go to Fort Smith a couple of days before them boys start play-ing arson anyway."

"And you didn't find anything to eat?"

He dug a clumsily wrapped packet from his livery pocket and untied it. Six flat squares, slate-colored and pricked with cracker holes, lay inside.

Saranell picked one up. It had the consistency of stone. "What is it?"

"Hardtack. It come in mighty handy for traveling." He took it from her and returned it to the package. "It ain't a delicacy, mind you, but we lucky that when I locate a soldier willing to part with some of them rock-hard crackers, them Yankees already been by and supply us with forty U.S. dollars."

"You paid forty dollars for six crackers!"

"Ain't nobody exchanging food for money these days even if somebody got something like this here iron biscuit to exchange."

He looked down at her forlorn expression. "But we can save them army crackers for when we get on the road. Joseph gather up some of that flour off the ground, and he let me take some." He carefully extracted a kerchief from another pocket and showed it to her. The flour in the cloth was no larger than the size of her fist. "While I make us a pancake, why don't you take a silver pitcher and pick some of them jonquils coming up through the snow. Maybe they cheer your mama up some."

"Didn't you notice that it's cold outside?" She stayed seated on the carpet.

"Them yellow blooms coming up hale and hearty. You bound to be as sturdy as some peaked little flower. Go on now. Something cheerful be good for your mama with her cough and all."

She sighed.

But at last she got up and threw on the gray cloak.

"Don't forget the pitcher." He held it out to her.

"It's icy cold."

She nonetheless took it, trudged out the back door, and started gathering jonquils from beside the brick path.

"Maybe Renny's right. Maybe Mama will like some flowers," she murmured as she stooped for the yellow blooms. "But I'd like them better if they were pokeweed we could eat."

She tucked the stems into the mouth of the pitcher, and when she couldn't crowd any more in, she took it back inside.

Geneva didn't acknowledge the bouquet, however, and she ate the third of tasteless pancake without a comment. Only when Saranell brought in the packet of hardtack and showed her did she laugh. "It's just as well Tawny took off, isn't it? Six crackers divide more easily by three than by four."

A cough interrupted her, but while she coughed, she said to Renny, "We may as well start tomorrow. There's not a thing for us here, and it'd be a shame to let Fanny entertain all the generals by herself."

"Yes'm."

And at dawn, Toby pulled the coach down the avenue of Rosegate's oaks as if he'd been waiting for years to be in the shafts of a carriage. Geneva, bundled in quilts and all the lap robes but the one she left for Saranell, stared ahead as if she missed neither the bays nor her maid.

The little mule was naturally slower than the two matched carriage horses, however, and it took them an hour to reach the edge of town. But finally, the landau rolled past the blackened poles of what had been elms, the blackened bricks of what had once been townhouses, the college, and the Episcopal church. Snow lay in the shadows of the debris and over the twists of fused iron fencing.

Saranell stared from one side of the street to the other.

If she'd been alone in the carriage with Renny, she'd have pointed out burned items she recognized—charred wooden beds, pianos, pie safes—and she'd have urged him to hypothesize about the melted nuggets of things she could no longer identify.

But since she wasn't alone with Renny, and since Geneva said no more about the loss of the church or the stage office than she'd said about the loss of her horses and her maid, Saranell kept quiet as well, and Toby pulled them in silence through the ruined town.

They passed no other carriage or other people, but as they reached the outskirts, Saranell cried, "Look, Mama!"

Three piled wagons stood beside what was left of a silo. One wagon had lost a wheel, and four women and a group of children and slaves huddled in the snow.

"Look, Mama, it's Mrs. Pate!"

Geneva gave them no more than a glance. "We're too far away to tell who it is. Maybe it's Naomi Pate. Maybe it isn't."

When Renny looked back from the driver's box, Geneva flicked her gloved hand with the ring. "Drive on."

"But that's Joseph. And there's Abby. I know it's Mrs. Pate, Mama."

"There's nothing we can do. And there's no use our stopping in this cold and getting in the way." She gazed at the winter landscape ahead rather than at the little group around the stalled wagons.

Saranell didn't try to argue any longer.

Finally, when the carriage was well around the next curve, Geneva murmured, "This whole war is so inconvenient, so ridiculous."

Sun eased through the high clouds, but a cold wind came up as the road took them into the hills. The wind shook Renny's beaver hat and whipped cold grit against Saranell's cheekbones as she gnawed the square of hardtack Renny passed back to her sometime in the afternoon.

Geneva looked at her square. "Since this will have to serve as both lunch and dinner, I suppose we need to eat it slowly," she said sarcastically.

Saranell didn't remind her there was no other way to eat the stony bread. She merely sucked on the square and watched snow-covered mountains replace the hills.

Mists gathered along the peaks and cliffs, and fog dropped into the valleys along the sides of the road.

Renny looked around at Geneva in her quilts. "The road getting mighty steep ahead, Miss Geneva, and the sun fixing to go down. They a inn up ahead, and we could maybe stop there for the night."

Geneva looked at him in moody silence, but at last, when they'd almost reached the entrance drive to the inn, she said, "Oh, all right. I suppose we may as well stop."

She didn't look at the shabby buildings or at the equally shabby refugees who squatted around small fires in the courtyard as Renny stopped the carriage near the inn porch.

He jumped from the driver's box and handed Geneva down. Then he went back, took one of the bundles from the carriage floor, and as soon as he set Saranell on the steps beside her mother, he went around behind the building.

Under ordinary circumstances, Saranell would have been thrilled to be able to spend the night in what the sign over the door called the "Wayfarers' Tavern," and she'd have shown keen interest in the other travelers—some of them children who might have been her age—crowding the yard and hunching beneath the overhang of the porch. But since the circumstances were far from ordinary, and since it was clear that Geneva didn't wish to recognize anyone fleeing their town, going the same direction they were headed, Saranell carefully didn't gaze directly at anyone either until Renny came back and informed them that he'd managed to bargain a large silver tray and a pitcher for a closet-like room with a bed for Geneva and a pallet for Saranell.

She followed her mother inside, and because no meals could be had for any amount of barter, they hurried at once to the tiny room while Renny went to sleep in the carriage.

For a change, Geneva awoke early the next morning, and by dawn, they were once more wrapped in their quilts and on their way.

Saranell didn't point out the tents or the camps along the snowy sides of the road, and when the carriage overtook a loaded dogcart pulled by a milk cow, she didn't try to see if the owner had once been a neighbor.

Toby trudged on, the sky clouded, they slowly ate the last three squares of hardtack, and Saranell was lulled by the carriage sway and her mother's cough.

It was well into the afternoon before a shout jolted her awake. "Whoa!"

The carriage dipped into a hollow of the road, and Renny braced against the reins as Toby skidded in the snow-slush mud. "Whoa!"

A heavy wagon suddenly loomed on the hill and sped down toward them.

Neither Renny nor the other driver could stop or swerve in time. Toby crashed into the horse, a strawberry roan who gave a terrified whinny and reared.

"Watch out!" Renny reined the little mule back from the hooves, but both the roan and Toby pitched to the ground amid a tangle of harnesses and bridles. Saranell jerked her hands from the rim of the landau as it slammed into the side of the wagon.

She and Geneva tumbled into each other, and silver pieces clanged.

"Look what you done!" Renny shouted at the wagon driver.

"I—I couldn't see nobody on the road from the top of that hill." The driver's voice cracked as if he were about to burst into tears. "I come up to the crest, and I couldn't see below in the gully."

Renny glanced up, then down quickly to the entangled roan and mule.

For the driver wasn't a servant but a young blond soldier, in his early teens, clad in jean trousers and a butternut jacket. His right arm had been thrust through his jacket sleeve, but the left cuff dangled over a filthy bandage that may or may not have contained a complete arm. "Please, ma'am," he said as he saluted and the empty sleeve flapped. "I got to get to Fayetteville."

Geneva coughed. "Fayetteville has been burned to the ground."

The boy stared at her helplessly. "I—I can't—" He choked. "I can't be on the road another night with them." He pointed but didn't look at the wagon bed behind him.

Saranell raised up to peer into it.

Men lay in a single row, packed shoulder-to-shoulder between the plank sides that contained them. A dusting of snow covered them, and their faces all looked alike.

Their skin had stiffened, and although some eyelids had been closed, most pairs of eyes stared blankly at the sky. Every set of teeth hung partially agape.

They wore a patchwork of clothing, but enough butternut tan jackets and caps were scattered among them to identify the wagonload as Confederate dead.

And as Saranell looked down at them, one corpse seemed familiar.

"I heard the army's got a hospital in Cane Hill. Do you know if that's true, ma'am?" the boy was saying brokenly. "I can go there if they ain't no place left in Fayetteville to take them."

Geneva inspected the wagon coldly. "I don't think these men need a hospital."

Renny helped the horse and the little mule to their feet while he moved his hands over their flanks and legs. "You all right," he assured them both.

Then he climbed onto the carriage box without looking at the boy soldier again and turned Toby aside.

The landau lurched away from the load of corpses.

The wagon driver knuckled his forelock of dishwater hair, and the reins slapped his pale nose. "Thank you, ma'am," he said for no reason.

Saranell grabbed the edge of the carriage and stood looking at the wagon. As it slid behind them, she gave a small gasp of recognition as she kept her gaze locked on the dead bodies in the wagon bed.

The dead eyes of Early Yarborough stared back at her.

12

SHE SANK INTO the carriage seat. "Those are Papa's men," she said. "Nonsense."

Saranell felt for Madison amid the quilts. "They were, Mama. One of them was Mr. Yarborough. Remember Papa wrote that Mr. Yarborough lost all his goods during that battle and joined the Arkansas Fourteenth." She didn't remind her mother that Early Yarborough had sold them Renny. "Mr. Yarborough's body is in that wagon."

"Your father's nowhere near here. He'd have come by if he were."

"Mr. Yarborough was in Papa's troop."

But before Saranell could insist any further, Geneva said, "We're stopping at the stage relay station. You can ask if there's a letter." She nodded toward a white building on a snowy crest ahead. "At least no one seems to have burned it yet."

The station, surrounded by white outbuildings, fences, and corrals, was farther away than it looked, however, and twilight had spread across the horizon before the carriage got near enough for them to see that horses milled in the corral.

"Do you think those are Yankee horses, Mama?"

Geneva frowned before the tip of her gloved finger smoothed the frown. "Well, if the Yankees have that many horses, they won't need to confiscate our mule, will they? We'll stop."

Renny nodded and turned into the muddy yard.

The fences had been mended and whitewashed, but the abandoned stagecoaches in the yard might have been left to decay decades earlier.

"Get close," Geneva rasped. "And bring in my teapot and the ground acorns. I don't care if the place is full of Yankees. I shall still act in a civilized manner."

Saranell jumped down with Madison and followed her mother inside.

A round-bellied man, wearing a red stocking cap with a tassel swinging from its knitted point, ran to meet them. A crowd of men in uniforms sat around an oak table close to the fire.

The uniforms had all been dyed with the faulty butternut dye of the Confederacy, and as Geneva came through the door, the men leapt to their feet.

Geneva gave an elaborate curtsey in their direction. "I want a room for the night," she said to the round innkeeper. She stood grand and serene, her cough momentarily controlled.

"My rooms is full up right now, ma'am." He bowed and the tail of his cap swung back and forth. "But I can see if one of the gentlemen—"

A chorus from the men interrupted him with offers of rooms, and Geneva beamed at the collection of gray uniforms.

"My servant is bringing in coffee—acorn coffee, of course, for the war effort—" She smiled. "But if y'all would care to join me—"

Another chorus of "yeses" swept the table.

"We have some hardtack, ma'am," one of the officers said gallantly. "We'd be mighty honored if you'd share it with us."

"How kind." She untied her bonnet and moved toward the table where, with a scraping of boots and chair legs, she was heartily welcomed.

Saranell sat down in one of the vacated chairs beside her mother and watched the tin plate of hardtack pass around. It was obvious that her mother wasn't going to ask the men if they knew anything about the Arkansas Fourteen. She probably wasn't going to ask if there was a letter.

"Have one of these biscuits if you got good strong teeth, ma'am," one man was saying cheerfully.

Geneva pulled off a glove and accepted a square. She didn't bite into it, however, but put it beside the limp glove and murmured, "I hope y'all are chasing Yankees. I had to leave my plantation because of them."

"We are, ma'am." The officer beside her smiled. "But remember, they do have more men than we've got."

Geneva flirted and smiled and was in the midst of an amusing account of leaving her house at Balm-of-Gilead when Renny brought in the silver teapot and the canister of parched ground acorns.

Saranell no longer tried to listen to the conversation. She tucked her own piece of hardtack in her jumper pocket so she could share it with Renny later and let her gaze swing between the fire and the red-capped stationmaster who bustled in and out with a great soot-covered teakettle of boiling water and a clatter of tin cups.

"Y'all must taste this special wartime blend," Geneva cried gaily as she let the acorns steep in her silver teapot.

Saranell held fast to Madison to keep her eyelids from drooping.

But it was no use, and at last she sagged into the wooden chair and laid her head on the wooden table.

When she opened her eyes gray light filled the room.

Her neck was stiff as she raised her head.

It was morning, and she still sat at the table with her mother and the ring of Confederate officers. The fire in the fireplace blazed as it had the night before.

Geneva seemed more flushed but even more pleased with herself and the company than she'd been when Saranell fell asleep. She was laughing her trilling laugh.

"I wish we could accompany you to Fort Smith, ma'am, but we got to start after those Yankees, who are going in the opposite direction."

"Of course you do. The sooner you wipe them off the face of the map, the sooner we can all go home." She coughed lightly, then said to Saranell, "Now that you're awake, dear, go find Renny and have him bring the carriage around. There wasn't a letter waiting here from your father." She dimpled at the officers and men. "I thank y'all for a most charming evening. You can't know how relieved I felt when I found that those horses outside belonged to our men."

Saranell pushed back her chair and, with Madison, clumped across the greasy floor to a door that opened into the yard.

The mud had frozen into hard ruts during the night.

A dense fog made it difficult for her to weave toward the shape of a barn, and she stumbled against the hardened clay.

"Renny!" She finally reached the barn, which reeked of molding hay.

Renny had already harnessed Toby. "I been wondering when you and your mama be ready to start."

Saranell stroked Toby's nose. "I think she wants to make Fort Smith by nightfall."

He looked out the door. "Maybe if them white billows of fog burn off by noon."

An odor of rotting straw drifted through the cold air.

Saranell fondled the velvety mule ears. "When we get to Fort Smith maybe Toby can have some oats and some good hay."

"Now don't go filling this mule's head with no fantasy lies. You ought to know nobody in Fort Smith be likely be to have fodder. Soldiers been there, too, remember."

"But not Yankee troops. Mama says our soldiers are more considerate than the Yankees. Our soldiers aren't thieves."

Renny snorted.

She frowned. "What does that mean?"

He shrugged.

"The Yankees stole Tawny."

"Taking Tawny ain't exactly like taking a sack of grain. And she ain't protesting much while she ride away with them Yankees as I remember."

"Well, they paid ten times less than Papa paid for the bays." When he didn't say anything to that, she added, "A Confederate officer wouldn't have cheated like that. A Southerner would have known how much a good horse was worth."

"Maybe."

"Confederate officers are gentlemen."

"But with all this war disruption, they also mighty poor gentlemen."

"What does that mean?"

"It mean that sometime last night, when I ain't inside here with the carriage, one of them fine Southern gentlemen reach in a gunny sack and filch a silver sugar bowl."

But then he went on softly, "But you don't need to be mentioning that to your mama. She have a pleasurable time talking to them officers, and since we ain't got no sugar, we ain't needing no sugar bowls just yet."

13

AMID THE GRAY-CLAD OFFICERS, Geneva had managed to control her illness, but as soon as the parties separated, the carriage left the stagecoach station, and the fog closed over them like a white porcelain tureen lid, Geneva's will flagged, her face flushed, and her yellow eyes glittered with fever.

The carriage bounced and jolted against the frozen mud while an unseen Toby dragged them up unseen heights and down into invisible valleys in the thick white foam. The sky, the road, and the mountains disappeared into the mist.

Saranell had climbed onto the driver's box with Renny, and now she peered hard at the reins leading into white nothingness. "How much farther to Fort Smith?"

"Too far. Your mama getting worse in this damp cold. We got to stop and let her rest some."

He clicked his tongue as if a mule actually were attached to the ends of the leather strands disappearing into the fog bank. "You watch them trees on each side." He raised his voice as if the whiteness were going to swallow his words.

"What am I looking for?"

"Rooftop. Maybe a chimney."

Fog muffled them in a moist white blanket.

A juniper branch jutted from the cloud bank, slid back into the milky blankness again.

Geneva coughed, shoved aside the quilts as her fever rose, gathered them close around her throat again as the chills took over.

Saranell tensed and stared ahead.

Suddenly the fog veil shredded. Toby became visible, and a brick chimney loomed ahead.

Saranell grabbed Renny's livery sleeve, pointed, and he nodded.

As the fog thinned, thickened, thinned again, the chimney appeared and disappeared.

126

Saranell held her breath and strained forward. She clasped the sides of the little gray cape together and crossed her arms over her chest for warmth.

At last the carriage made a turn into what could have been a driveway, and the little mule stopped beside the chimney.

Below the column of bricks lay blackened ruins where the walls of the house had stood.

"We're too late. Somebody already burned it," Saranell said. "We can't stay here." She huddled sadly on the driver's box while the fog swirled around her.

Then Renny straightened and pointed. "They another building yonder. Maybe we still be able to spend the night after all."

He urged Toby forward, and the little hooves picked among the rubble until they came to the trunk of a fallen tree. The little mule whinnied and refused to budge.

"Okay, mule." Renny lowered the reins. "I guess this as far as we ride on this driveway."

"I'll go see if the house has a roof." She slipped from the box.

"Don't be rushing into no—" Renny called after her, but she hurried through the clinging white mist to what appeared to be a low, square house. The walls were stacked, chinked logs.

Renny was suddenly beside her.

"No telling who or what be in there." He stepped in front of her and they approached the log cabin together.

Renny shoved the door open with his foot.

The cabin was empty. It was without a single window, but it had walls and a roof, and a huge stone fireplace took up one entire side of the room.

"We can have a fire!" Saranell shouted as she hopped inside.

"If *we* get us some wood." He grinned at her. "Come tote in them covers so your mama can rest."

The fog had tightened, and everything beyond Saranell's outstretched hand became invisible as she followed Renny closely back to the carriage beside the fallen tree.

He didn't offer his glove to help Geneva down this time but merely lifted her and carried her toward the log shelter. Saranell gathered the quilts and lap robes and sped to the cabin behind them.

The open door let in enough light to see, and she stood just inside and blinked around.

The floor was dirt, and the furniture consisted of a bed, a table, one chair, and a wall shelf nailed to a log.

Geneva had sunk into the chair, her face gray with fatigue.

"Get a fire going good and this be one cozy place," Renny said to Saranell. "Go fetch a cedar branch to sweep out them ashes while I hide old Toby and that carriage under some trees. No use to let somebody passing catch sight of our coach and our mule. No use to tempt somebody."

She tucked Madison into her jumper sash, adjusted the cloak around them both, and went obediently outside.

She felt her way along a stand of junipers just beyond the log cabin and tore at a limb. But the branch was too green to break or twist off, and she moved to the next tree, then the next, to try again. After bending and tugging at a few more stubborn limbs, she gave up and looked around for Renny and his knife.

He was nowhere in sight.

But a spot of scarlet glimmered through the fog, and she hurried toward it.

The whiteness became a solid ball, and she put her head down to filter the wet fog from her nostrils as she broke through the snow.

Ice crystals filled her shoes, and she stared down at the snow.

When she looked back up, nothing moved in the fog.

"Renny!"

Whiteness deadened the sound.

"I thought we were closer to the cabin than this," she said to Madison. She listened, then raised her voice again. "Renny!"

She took another step and slid into icy water that immediately filled her shoes and washed against her skirt and stockings.

She gasped, and her temples pounded.

The fog had sheltered a pond, and she stood in cold water and silt up to her knees.

As mist raked the surface of the pool, her hand dove to her sash to rescue Madison's red cotton boots from the water.

Then she flailed her arms to pull her sodden skirt, cape, and slave brogans free. She threw herself backward, and the shoes sucked against the mud but stayed on her feet as she freed herself from the shallows.

"There wasn't a pond between the carriage and the cabin." The blood in her temples thudded again. "We're lost, Madison."

She twisted around to stare behind her.

Nothing but whiteness clung to her.

Her throat closed, but she managed to shout, "Renny!"

She clutched Madison as a talisman and yelled. Mist collected on her face and dripped into her mouth as she opened it. "Renny!"

Her shout bounced against the fog crystals as her yells became strangely exalted, strangely joyful. "Renny!"

She threw back her head, closed her eyes, and howled into the interior of the white globe.

"Renny! Renny!"

Her wet skirt and cloak, her soaked stockings were turning her to a column of ice, but she didn't stamp her feet or move in the fog and snow as she shouted.

"Renny! Renny!"

A hand abruptly closed over her arm.

14

RENNY LOOMED beside her. "How come you clear down here? I about to decide I ain't locating you before dark."

"Where's the cabin?"

"Over that way." He directed her. "I just about to give up when old Toby prick up them mule ears of his. He either hear a pack of Yankees or a pack of wolves or you." He shuffled her through the snow powder with a hand on her shoulder. "So I head over here and come on you shouting up a storm."

In a minute, the edge of a log corner scattered the fog, and in another, she stood before a fire blazing in the huge hearth.

"I find her about a mile away," Renny said to Geneva, who lay in the bed buried under the quilts.

She may have nodded, but her movements beneath the mounded quilts were too faint in the firelight for Saranell to tell. No fever now colored her pale face, and since she'd removed the scarlet traveling outfit and the scarlet bonnet, no reflected tint rouged the thick glaze of sweat on her face.

"It's cold in here," Saranell said. She sat down and dragged off her stockings.

"If I ain't searching around in the fog for somebody who ain't using the sense they born with, it might be warmer," Renny said.

But he didn't sound angry as he knelt to feed lengths of gray cedar, that had obviously come from a worm fence, into the fire. And when he handed Saranell a towel with Fanny Culver's monogram and said, "Dry off them feet so you don't catch your death," he sounded more worried than irritated.

He set the sodden brogans on the stone ledge of the hearth and draped the wet stockings across them.

The cedar flames bounced higher, and Saranell rubbed the towel over her feet and ankles. Then she put her hand in her pocket for the hardtack from the night before.

It was gone.

She turned a stricken face toward Renny. "I lost the piece of hard-tack I was saving to divide with you."

"Never mind." He produced one of the gray squares and handed it to her while he took up a warmed quilt. "I got two from the station. I ate mine, so you eat this one." He tucked the quilt around her.

She relaxed in the coverlet as her teeth gnawed the bread, and when she finished the hard biscuit, she settled her head on a fold of quilt.

When she opened her eyes, Renny was kneeling before the hearth beside her.

"Did I fall asleep?" she whispered.

Renny's teeth gleamed. "For maybe fifteen hours."

She stared. "Is it night out?"

"Night and nearly morning again."

"Are we starting for Fort Smith when it gets light?"

He shook his head. "You mama having bad spells of them chills and fevers, and she need some good hard rest."

"Oh." She looked around the room. After a moment she asked, "Was this the servants' quarters?"

She didn't compare it to the tiny servants' huts at Balm-of-Gilead.

"Keep your voice down," Renny said softly. "No. It belong to the overseer most likely. Slave quarters off that way, but they been burnt down like the main house. Barn and stables gone too. But I guess who-ever set them fires ain't got the time to set this cabin ablaze. It take more than ordinary piddling fire to burn logs."

He meditated on the thick log walls before he went out for more wood.

Saranell studied her slave brogans, whose leather toes had curled.

"Of course I knew you'd come," Geneva said suddenly in her usual voice with her usual mocking laugh.

Saranell jumped.

"I told you he rode straight up to my papa's veranda and dropped that pearl ring in my lap." She paused and might have been listening for a reply. "I *will* marry him if you don't propose. I can have an heir, too, you know."

131

"Mama?" Sarnell unbundled from her quilt and hurried to the bed in her bare feet.

Geneva's gold eyes stared at the wavering shadows against the logs. "You know you don't love her, Haze. You know perfectly well you love me."

"Mama?"

Geneva started.

Then her topaz eyes stared around the room before they returned to Saranell. "Are we ready to start?"

"Renny says we need to wait a little longer."

Geneva's hair clung to her forehead with the strength of illness. She gave a cough and wiped her upper lip with the quilt.

She coughed again hard, and was still coughing when the door opened and Renny came in happily.

"Look-ee here!" He carried something in the flap of his crimson jacket, and as he bent down, he let a dozen white objects the size of fists roll over the hearth stones.

"I see a sink up by the ruins of the barn." He picked up one of the lopsided white balls, and using the end of a log, shoved it under the ashes. "Lots of things make a mound, but you got to bury something in the ground to make a sinkhole in the snow."

Saranell moved to watch him as he took up the balls one at a time and poked them into the ashes.

"I dig down until I come on a patch of straw, and look-ee here. Turnips." The last ball disappeared under the ashes as Geneva stopped coughing. "Enough for a good mouthful apiece."

He scooted the remaining fence rails toward Saranell and unwound effortlessly from the hearth stones. "Wood go clean out my mind when I see them turnips, so now I got to get us some more to cook our dinner. I be right back, Miss Geneva, with a bowl to melt you some snow so you can have a nice cool drink."

He looked down and gestured at Saranell. "You sit here and lay on one piece of wood at a time. Keep the fire making them ashes so we can keep cooking."

Saranell knelt down.

"Don't be falling asleep on the job now."

She glowered at him, but he was grinning as he turned away.

She watched the door open and close to blue sky, then reached for a log.

Only the sound of the fire riffled around the room for a long moment.

Then Geneva murmured, "All that ridiculous pride, Haze. All that ridiculous waste of time." She coughed, sighed, and fell silent.

Saranell looked up, but she didn't move from the fire.

The dry fence logs burned in quick bursts that showered cinders against the interior of the fireplace, and Saranell carefully put on length after length. She glanced at Madison leaning against the stones, then toward Geneva. "Cedar burns so fast."

Geneva didn't stir.

Soon only one piece of fencing remained.

Then the door opened again.

"It's about time. Do you think the turnips are done yet?" Saranell looked over her shoulder.

But it wasn't Renny who stepped into the firelight.

It was a tow-headed soldier wearing an overcoat of dark blue.

He was leveling a pistol at her as he closed the door behind him.

15

"WELL, NOW ain't this something."

The soldier looked from Saranell to the bed. "A little girl and a woman out here all by theirselves."

The bed creaked, and Geneva dragged herself upright in the nest of quilts on the bed.

The man lacked a cap and gloves, his shoes were hide wrappings held on with rope, and as he shrugged off the blue greatcoat, he revealed a gray worsted shirt and homespun jean trousers held up by brown suspenders.

"You know how long it's been since I laid eyes on anything female that wasn't a horse or a cow or a hundred years old?" He dropped the greatcoat to the dirt floor.

Geneva lifted her chin. "I trust that you Yankees are civilized enough to—"

"Hell, I ain't no Yankee. That there's a captured coat." The steady round eye of the pistol turned to Geneva. "Come over here. You the overseer's missus?"

"How ridiculous." But the effort of sitting up and rasping out her scorn brought on a spasm of coughing.

"Papa is—" Saranell began.

The man didn't look at her but kept his gaze on Geneva. "Since you got such a bad cold—" he said as he stepped away from the greatcoat and started toward the bed, "—no need to stir. Nor to talk none with that cough neither. A woman don't have to be a talker to please me."

Saranell sprang to her feet and threw herself against the homespun jean trousers and worsted shirt.

But her slight weight didn't budge the man, and the hand with the pistol flicked her away like a dry branch.

The blow sent her spinning into the fireplace stones, and as she tried to catch herself, a dull snap thudded from her arm.

Pain sped from the center of the bone, and she plunged into a pool of pain and blackness as the man's voice said from far away, "You been waiting here for me. Ain't that right?"

Other sounds filled the inky water as Saranell slowly sank.

She rose on a cold wave, floated just below the dark surface, sank again.

Time stopped, pounded back again as the wave of pain pushed her into the light.

The darkness split, and in the rent between the curtains of blackness, Renny stood with his arms piled high with wood and a silver bowl in one hand.

Saranell watched him from the depth of the cold pit.

The silver bowl and logs bounced lazily against the dirt, fringing dust into the air as Renny floated out of the circle of light and away from Saranell's contained view.

Then the soldier in the gray shirt sailed slowly, without a sound, toward the cabin wall.

Sound abruptly returned as the back of the soldier's blond head cracked against the logs.

He lay stunned a few seconds before he shook his head and put out a hand to pull himself up.

"Stay!" Renny moved into Saranell's sight again. From his tone, he might have been commanding a dog.

Now it was Renny who held the pistol, which he aimed at the man's face.

Beneath the smoky-blond hair, the soldier's eyes soaked up the firelight, and he stared at Renny with astonishment. "What'd you say, boy?"

"You heard me fine."

"You better call me 'sir,' boy, if you know what's good for you." He again leaned on his hand and started to get up.

"You move from that spot and I blow out what brains you got left—sir," Renny said.

The throb of Saranell's arm respread the black eclipse, but she fought it back and kept her eyelids fixed wide. Without moving her head, she cut her gaze from the blond man to Renny.

"You struck a white man, boy, a soldier of the Confederacy. That's a hanging offense." He looked toward the door and his threat stopped. His stained teeth parted in a triumphant grin.

Outlined against the morning sky, another soldier, wearing a gray cap and gray trousers under a blue greatcoat, held a rifle fitted with a long, glittering bayonet.

He held it unwaveringly on Renny.

"What's going on here, Tray?"

"You got here just in time." The first soldier now lunged upright and brushed at his trousers. "This here buck tackled me soon as I walked in."

He moved past Saranell, and from the shelter of his fellow soldier with the bayonet, he shut the door and barked to Renny, "Put that gun down now, boy, or we'll quarter you before we hang you."

Renny gazed impassively at the two men as he lowered the pistol. He kept his finger on the trigger.

"Saw smoke coming from a chimney while I was back in them woods and I thought a runaway might be holed up in here." The soldier called Tray jerked his thumb at the room. "Found the overseer's missus and kid." He started toward Renny. "And look at them good boots on this here runaway."

His fist arched out, but a scarlet sleeve blocked the swing, and Renny shoved him backward.

He tripped over a piece of wood and danced to keep upright. "Why you—"

"Give it a rest, Tray," the other man snapped.

He stood thin, pointing the rifle and bayonet with twig fingers while he swerved his thin neck between Saranell and Renny. "What happened here?"

A juniper log exploded, and the two men jumped, but Renny said over the scattering embers, "That soldier, he—" He stopped, gestured toward the bed, then turned to Saranell. "I think the child here got a broke arm."

The tall man went over to the bed, stooped beside it, and his sapling ankles showed under the edge of the greatcoat. His bare feet were stuffed into battered shoes, and he moved them uncomfortably as he uttered a soft oath.

Then he was kneeling beside Saranell in a halo of cold air.

In the firelight, eggshell blue eyes stared from a narrow skull that could have been hacked from the gray fencing. "You the overseer's little girl, missy?"

"Papa's a colonel in the Arkansas Fourteenth." The throb in her arm halted the words.

"A cock-and-bull story from a lying brat and a runaway ain't—"

"Renny's not a runaway."

"Like I say, you can't take no account from a—"

The tall soldier towered upright again. "I guess you should of pulled up them suspenders and put your coat back on before I got here, Tray, if you wanted me to believe you was jumped the minute you walked in the cabin."

He bent over Saranell once more, shoved his gray cap back from the bone forehead, reached out, and pulled her arm toward him.

The fierce jar of pain instantly blackened the room.

16

SHE OPENED HER EYES to the skeletal man still holding her arm, but now he was binding it tight between two slabs of wood. He'd been muttering, but the words stopped as he glanced up to see her awake. "Now, don't that feel better?"

She lay on a quilt pallet close to the fire, and a blue Yankee overcoat covered her with thick, wool warmth.

The fire had been built up, and the dusty-blond trooper sagged against the wall in nearly the spot where Renny had flung him. His hands lay palm-up on the dirt floor, and his feet in their wadding and twine stuck straight out before him. Nothing about him moved except for his eyes, which kept shifting from his fellow soldier to the walls.

Saranell looked past him. "Where's Renny?"

The thin blue-eyed soldier continued to circle the splint and her arm with heavy string. "Lay back now until I finish. Your boy's all right."

"Where is he?"

"He's all right. He's just outside."

"Renny only hit that man to protect Mama. Ask her. She can tell you he was only trying to—"

"He's all right. Your mama don't need to be talking." His bony hand tied off his bandaging and patted the binding. "See, now ain't that better?"

His gentle pat stirred the ache, but as he took his hand away, the pain stopped. She blinked hard and nodded.

"Just keep your arm in them slats. Raise up a bit." He tied a checkered red handkerchief at the back of her neck to form a sling and gently laid her arm in it.

"But why isn't Renny inside where it's warm?"

"He'll be back in a minute."

She opened her mouth, but before she could demand that he produce Renny at once, the cabin door swung back and Renny walked in.

The thin soldier looked up at him. He unwound his bony length and got to his feet. He took his own captured Yankee greatcoat from a peg on the wall and slid his long arms into the sleeves. Then he took up the rifle and bayonet he'd leaned against the fireplace. "All right, Tray. Let's go."

The tow-headed soldier made no effort to get up.

"I said, let's go."

The man's gaze made another quick circuit of the room. "Remember, I give up my gun to you voluntarily, McAndrews. So as not to cause no trouble. It ain't sensible for us to quarrel out here on patrol. We got to stick together, don't we?"

"You wasn't holding the gun when I come in if I recollect correctly."

"He hit a white man," the man on the floor said. "And you know the word of a slave ain't got no legal—"

"I don't need his word," the tall soldier said curtly. He motioned again with the bayonet for the man to stand.

"How was I to know they wasn't overseer trash?" he whined. "You hear how the boys talk about hired women. Trash ain't no account. They was here in this cabin all by theirselves where no decent women would of been. How was I to know?"

He gathered up his knees and hugged them. "You know I got a right to be took to Colonel Harrell. It's the law. I got the right to a trial or one a them court martials. I let you put me under arrest, and you have to—"

"I ain't got the strength to search out Colonel Harrell." The man rubbed a bone hand over his bone forehead. "And even if I found him, Colonel Harrell ain't the one who'd be next to you in a skirmish, having to depend on you to do the right thing, having to shoot Yankees to save your hide."

"But you just can't—"

"Your hide ain't worth saving."

He dropped to one knee beside Saranell again as if he's spilled a sack of bones. "Your ma's resting, and I dislike waking her, but you tell her I'm mighty sorry about—" He made a show of adjusting the kerchief on her arm. "You tell her I done what I had to do, and that Tray ain't ever going to—" He blinked blue eyes veined red with fatigue. "You take care of that arm now."

He unflexed with ladder swiftness.

He stared down at the other soldier while his mouth thinned with disgust.

Then he reached out with one thin hand and hauled the man to his feet.

"Let me go, McAndrews. I swear I'll light out for the Territory. Please!"

McAndrews dragged him across the room, pushed open the cabin door, and shoved him outside.

"I'm under arrest. You got a duty." The whine became a desperate wail. "Take me to Colonel Harrell! Please!"

The door shut on his plea.

Renny stirred the fire.

Saranell relaxed against the pallet and stared into the blaze with him.

After a long silence, what might have been a shot and a faint cry, or perhaps an animal scream, came from the distance and Saranell glanced at Renny's profile.

He didn't move, and her gaze lazily turned back to the cedar flames and the warm coat covering her.

She started and lifted her chin from the blue collar. "The soldier left his Yankee coat."

Renny gazed impassively into the fire.

"Renny, that soldier didn't take his coat to go out in the snow!" she repeated.

He put another log on the blaze. "He ain't likely to need it," he said at last.

17

RENNY HANDED SARANELL a turnip, which had no other flavor than scorch, but she ate it. And when Renny held out another, she took it, and chewed and swallowed it between intervals of pain and numbness and sips of melted snow from the silver serving dish.

The Yankee coat smelled of wood and smoke and horse hide as she snuggled into it and closed her eyes.

She awoke to a whisper and the discomfort of wooden slats against her side.

"—to Tyler."

Saranell cautiously raised her head.

Tyler.

Only her mother would talk about Tyler, Texas, but the ghostly whisper in the room couldn't belong to her mother.

Her gaze circled the walls, the table, chair and bed, the dancing shadows.

No one else was in the room except Renny, who stood beside the bed. The whisper must have existed in a dream.

"—as soon as you can."

No, the unearthly wheeze of words came from inside the cabin.

She carefully laid aside the Yankee great coat. Pain shot through her arm, and the dirt floor danced with the firelight.

More knife-sharp words, "—her Aunt Nora—until after the war— Send a message—" wavered around the walls.

She braced herself until the pain and the room settled again, then she struggled to her feet.

She waited again for the weaving logs of the cabin wall to steady before she tottered to the bed.

Renny stood at the side of the bed, but Saranell didn't recognize the figure in the bed, propped amid the quilts.

The face, surmounted by strands of lank hair, was a distorted mask. Glistening tiger eyes peered from empurpled eye sockets and stared at Saranell.

Saranell wanted to say her mother's name, but she couldn't frame it before the mask-like face.

A few seconds went by.

Then the mask said, "I wasn't fair to your father. I shouldn't have married him." The voice was more like a scraping against hard wood with a file, and the wound of a mouth didn't seem to move. "Such a ridiculous—waste of years." The swollen tongue may have tried to swallow. "For us all."

The head of the figure pressed slowly into the folded quilt that served as a pillow and the matted hair sank against the patchwork pattern as if lowering into stone.

"If Haze had only—"

The words, that were only vaguely sounds, stopped again, and a glint of satisfaction kindled in the eyes. The battered, unrecognizable features waited as if for some expected news, and then one white hand snaked from the quilts. It lifted, stiffened in a gesture of warning and curled into a fist.

The fingers became a talon that grasped at empty air.

Then the hand dropped to the quilt with the finality of a rock.

The eyelids behind the mask closed, reopened, tried to close again, but hung partly ajar. The lungs beneath the coverlet inflated, exhaled, inflated again, and held.

The long seconds lengthened, but the rib cage and the quilts didn't move again.

The white face aged like crumpled paper even as no muscle twitched.

The figure remained still.

"Your mama in a fine place now." Renny's fingers gently sealed the eyelids and held them shut. When he removed his hand, the long dark lashes lay youthful against the ancient cheeks.

He reached out with his other hand and turned Saranell's shoulder toward the pallet on the floor. "Now you get some rest."

The pain engulfed her as she lay down, but she didn't tell Renny.

He covered her carefully. "We got to start soon."

She tried to nod, but she couldn't manage it, and for a long time she lay suspended beneath the greatcoat in a dream state of pain, fire-light, and frost.

Then Renny's voice said quietly, "Now you hold Madison with your good hand."

She opened her eyes to daylight and let her lungs test the crisp air.

She lay packed in the carriage with the quilts and bundles.

Toby was stamping his hooves, swaying his head impatiently from the carriage shafts while Renny said, "Now, you look good at them trees and the cabin and the once-been house now. See them rocks?"

He pointed to a pile of stones, and she swiveled her gaze from the log cabin to the ruined house and the line of junipers. "Get it in your head good to show your papa when he come back."

She stared at the burned plantation, the gray collection of stones piled higher than the useless bricks of the house foundation.

"You sure you can find it again?"

"I think so."

"Thinking ain't good enough. Look close now at that cairn."

He eased her gently upright while she studied the site, and when she nodded at last, he let her sink back on the carriage cushions with Madison in the crook of her arm.

He climbed onto the driver's box, swaying the landau with his weight. "All right. You abide quiet in them covers now."

The charred timbers and the chimney bricks slid by, and her awareness slid into inattention. In the gentle motion of the ride, she let her eyelids droop.

This time, the world churned back and forth, and a grating whisper said, "I wasn't fair to your father–fair to your father. I shouldn't have married him. If Haze had only—If Haze had only—"

White fists like talons reached toward her through the speckled darkness, but Saranell rocked away.

"I wasn't fair to your father," the whisper repeated. "I wasn't fair. I shouldn't have married him."

Then other voices began to talk over the whisper.

The words ran together, flowed over her, getting louder and louder, and it was clear that a crowd had gathered.

"Be quiet. You'll wake Mama." She tried to say it with stern anger. "She needs to rest."

A towel with a rose-embroidered "FC" flapped at the noisy conversation.

Madison sat and watched with her blue-painted porcelain eyes.

This was no time for a party. Her mother needed to rest so they could go on to Fort Smith. How could Mrs. Culver have been so thoughtless?

Saranell tried to unglue her eyelids.

Her eyelids refused to cooperate.

She frowned and tried to tell the partygoers to be quiet, but her lips refused to part and shush them.

She tossed her head and moved her arms. The splints jabbed into her ribs, and the pain spurted over her. Her eyes sprang open.

Sunlight stabbed her pupils, and she blinked into full consciousness.

A ring of strangers stood around the landau in the dazzling light.

They were murmuring and staring fixedly down at her.

18

HER EYES SWERVED to the empty driver's box, and she sat up quickly.

Now the pain grabbed at both her arm and her head as she threw off the Yankee greatcoat. But she ignored the pain and clutched Madison.

"The little girl woke up," a man said from beside the carriage.

"She ain't dead after all."

"Of course she ain't dead. She look fine except for the broke arm."

The strangers surged closer. A large woman in widow's black murmured, "The poor little tyke."

Saranell stared at the unfamiliar faces. "Where's Renny?" she demanded.

But before the crowd could say anything, Renny's voice said, "Good. You finally come around and wake up."

Her head jerked toward him, and she watched him thread his way through the crowd. He carried himself with the faked slave humility she'd seen before at Gilead as he walked around Birdsong guests. He lowered his gaze, skirting the white people with a proper avoidance, edging through, not touching anyone, not seeming to have a purpose in the crowd, and only someone as noticing as Saranell would have seen that he was moving to the exact spot he meant to reach.

And now he said with false humbleness, "Look, Miss Saranell." He pointed beyond the crowd. "You at Mr. Fisk's store, just like I say you be in no time."

She looked over the heads of the strangers.

The carriage indeed sat braked in the street before a wooden storefront on which had been tacked a newly painted sign, *OPAL FISK, DRYGOODS.*

But the crowd had been silent long enough, and the chorus of inquiry began again. "This boy says he's your driver. Is that true, child?"

"What are you doing out here all by yourself, missy?"

"Where'd you come by that Yankee greatcoat?"

"How come you been traveling all alone?

Renny reached into the carriage and helped her unwrap herself from the quilts. "Miss Saranell on her way to Boggy Depot," he said humbly.

"I'm meeting Papa there," Saranell lied hastily, in case one of the strangers decided to challenge Renny.

If they began to answer their own questions, they might decide to detain her. Everyone knew that adults had a way of thinking they knew what was best for children, and one of the members of this crowd might take it in his head to carry her home with him until they checked out Renny's story.

"Papa's in command of the Arkansas Fourteenth," she added, tossing aside the covers. "He's sending me to Texas to stay with my Aunt Nora."

Her voice had the tinny sound of her half-truths, but no one in the crowd would know that if she stood up straight, kept her eyes boldly open, and went inside the store.

"How come your mama let you be out here at—?"

"Now that you woke up, Miss Saranell, you best get on with them transactions your papa want." Renny collected a sack from the carriage floor.

"We're lucky Mr. Fisk came here from Fayetteville. He'll know just what Papa wants."

She didn't speak directly to Renny or to anyone in the crowd, but she spoke with a confidence that seemed to satisfy them, and they began to move away from the carriage while she scrambled carefully down.

She cradled her arm in the red kerchief and followed Renny to the store.

Only the widow remained behind at the side of the carriage, shaking her head and repeating, "Poor little tyke."

Renny closed the shop door on the woman's murmur, and said in a low voice to Saranell, "Let me do the bargaining."

They walked to the far end of the store—that was an exact copy of the store Opal Fisk had owned in Fayetteville—where a man, thick-

146

necked and bulbous, sat in a rocking chair before a glass-topped counter.

Opal Fisk's great stomach showed that he was a wealthy man, even wealthy enough to afford a substitute to do his soldiering for him, and he'd hired young Jeff Lowery to join the Arkansas Fourteenth in his place. He'd bought the young man's uniform, boots, rifle, and kit, and when Jeff had been buried following the battle of Oak Hills—without the head no one could find after the cannon ball had sheered it off— Opal Fisk had sent the young man's mother a hundred Confederate dollars.

The shopkeeper now sat rocking with the steady beat of an overfed man while he watched them come through the dusk of the room. His rocker was centered on a braided rug, and his cousin, Quincy Drood, curled at the edge of the rug beside him.

Quincy Drood stared hard at Saranell and Renny as they got closer.

Suddenly he shouted gleefully, "Miss Saranell!" He waved his arms and his body swayed back and forth. "Look, Mr. Opal, it Saranell Birdsong."

The store owner ignored him and his eyes flickered toward the sack Renny carried, but he swerved his gaze away from it until they stopped before him. Then he muttered to Saranell, "So you the Birdsong girl?"

Before she could do more than nod, Renny went around Opal Fisk and his cousin and hefted the burlap onto the glass counter. "Colonel Birdsong send in some silver to negotiate for food."

Opal Fisk scowled as if he'd been called away from some important business—by a servant at that—but he nonetheless got up heavily from the rocker with a practiced lack of curiosity. "Well, since you here, we may as well see what you got."

Renny had packed the frivolous silver pieces in one sack, and he now transferred sterling wire baskets, bread servers, and slotted chestnut bowls from the sack to the counter.

"You got a good polish on them." Opal Fisk's fat hand caressed a basket handle.

Renny laid out sterling ice cream forks, strawberry forks, openworked jelly spoons, olive tongs, fruit knives, nut scoops, and dishes of all sizes until the glass of the countertop was crammed.

Quincy Drood hadn't moved from the floor, and he rocked back and forth, staring at Saranell with delight.

"That all?" Opal Fisk backed slightly away. "They got a blockade on the Mississippi River in case you ain't heard. Food is harder and harder to come by."

His eyes may have taken on a speculative, hungry look, but his lids hung too low over them for anyone to be certain.

"Everybody's trading what they can't eat for something they can. And everybody's coming to me with their goods."

"The child need cornmeal, rice, whatever you can spare, sir," Renny said. "She got a ways to go yet."

"I can't get much for plated stuff." He dismissed the countertop of silver. "They ain't no call for resale plate."

"It's all sterling," Saranell burst out. "Mama doesn't own plate."

"Women can't tell sterling from plate, missy," Opal Fisk said. "Offer them a fancy gew-gaw—" He touched a silver bon-bon dish. "—and it don't matter if the thing's plate or not."

"Mama never keeps plate, not even if it's a gift. She—"

"Colonel Birdsong send all this in for bargaining," Renny interrupted her outburst firmly, but he managed to sound meek.

"Of course, cheap flashy pieces like most of this ain't worth much in trade."

Renny put a hand on Saranell's shoulder and pressed. A muscle in his cheek twitched, but he stood with his eyes discretely lowered. "Colonel Birdsong be mighty grateful to you if you see your way to helping his child, Mr. Opal."

"This whole shebang might be worth two pounds of rice at most." He brushed some of the pieces aside and thudded a small bag onto the counter. "But I'm losing money on the deal."

Renny swept up the bag before Saranell could refuse it. "Thank you, sir."

He turned her around by her uninjured arm, pushed her toward the front of the store, and despite his care for the splints, he shoved her through the door.

In the sunlight, her voice exploded. "And I was worried that Papa hadn't paid for the Dickens book! Mr. Fisk knew that was sterling! He knew Mama would never—"

He dragged her away from the front of the store and lifted her into the carriage seat. "You just a little girl, but now you got the experience of running smack into wartime greed. It even worse than plain old peacetime avarice."

He laid the sack of rice beside Madison and tucked the last burlap bag of silver under the seat. "At least Mr. Opal Fisk ain't faking patriotism and the like. He ain't putting on no airs or no pretense. Ain't nothing at work with Mr. Opal Fisk but greed, and we can take it or leave it."

He climbed into the box and talked over his shoulder. "If we don't barter them candy dishes for two pounds of rice, then he just let us chew on pickle forks for nourishment."

"He's a hateful man."

"Naw. Just greedy. Don't be wasting no hate on something so fast bound in human nature as greed." He signaled Toby with the reins. "Now don't be thinking about it. Just you be resting so that arm heal straight."

Quincy Drood suddenly sprang from the alley. "Miss Saranell!"

Toby shied in alarm.

"Miss Saranell!" Quincy Drood bobbed to the side of the carriage. He carried a five-pound sack of cornmeal in both arms, and he blinked against the sunlight with a cavern toad expression. "Mr. Opal ain't figured right, Miss Saranell."

He wobbled his too-large head and laid the sack in the seat beside her.

Then from his jacket, a hand-me-down that had once belonged to a much fatter man, he carefully pulled out three eggs and placed them in Madison's skirt. From another pocket he took a small leather-bound volume. "I got you a reading book, too, Miss Saranell."

He put it into her good hand and scuttled back into the alley.

Saranell opened the book.

Pride and Prejudice by Jane Austen.

She glanced back at the empty alley. "I didn't get to thank him."

Renny urged Toby into a steady clip away from the store. "Old Quincy don't need you to say it. He know you grateful."

19

"WHERE ARE WE?"

Renny had talked without pausing from the time they left Fort Smith, resting his voice only when she fell asleep.

Now she awoke to midday sunlight and a pause in the carriage sway. She looked around and asked again, "Where are we?"

"Indian Territory. This the old stage road to Boggy Depot. Right after there a bit, we cross the Red River into Texas."

They were stopped in a valley at the side of what was hardly more than a wagon path. Renny stood flexing his arms next to Toby, who was munching new grass.

"Will we run into scalping Indians?"

"Naw. The Indians here ain't the scalping kind. These the ones that come over to the Territory with all they silk dresses and china and slaves."

"Indians have servants?"

He gave his snort. "They live a long time in Georgia raising cotton before they get run off and sent over here by white men coveting all them plantations. No planter, red or white, be able to grow good cotton without slave help."

In what might have been an effort to keep her mind off Geneva, he'd told her volumes of facts as they'd bounced along, and now Saranell didn't ask how he knew about Indians. Instead, she said, "Have we crossed the Arkansas River?"

"You see a river up ahead?" he said with a touch of his old irony. But then he added, "You been sleeping so fine when we get to the ferry to cross the Arkansas, I don't like to wake you. Rocking on water be a lot like lilting along in a carriage. Both make for good sleeping."

"But I've never been on a ferry."

"You never been *awake* on a ferry at any rate."

He looked at her disappointed expression. "But they another ferry to cross the Red River after we go through Boggy Depot. And the Red River more grand than the Arkansas."

"We're going to Tyler?"

"You got to be staying with your aunt until your papa get back."

He didn't mention Geneva, and he glanced around the little valley while he continued. "If you getting ready to eat, we could stop here a while. I could fix a couple of them eggs old Quincy supply. How you like your eggs? Over easy? Scramble? Poach? Maybe hard boil and then crumble on toast with cream sauce?"

"Yes."

"How about I fry them on a rock? Can you get yourself down from that coach while I gather up some dry sticks for a fire?"

She nodded and pushed aside her bundle of covers and the Yankee coat.

It took her longer than usual to maneuver over the side of the carriage, however, and Renny had returned with an armload of dry wood by the time she reached the ground.

And while she stood dizzily folding Madison into the sling, a horse and rider came over the top of the rise.

"Renny," she whispered urgently.

But he'd also looked up at the horseman on a black horse and had moved to the side of the carriage.

"Is it another Yankee?"

"Can't tell. He too far away yet."

She strained toward the approaching horse, which had four white feet and a small white blaze in its forehead. "Will he take Toby?"

"Most likely he be satisfied with them eggs."

As the rider got closer, his butternut jacket became clearer, and Saranell watched Renny retreat into his servant role.

"Morning, missy. What are you doing out here? You lost?" The man, a middle-aged man with a salt-and-pepper beard and a gray kepi with a yellow crown, reined in his white-stockinged horse. "You needing some help?"

She shook her head. "We're not lost. We're on our way to meet

Papa." And before the soldier could ask, she volunteered, "Papa commands the Arkansas Fourteenth. Do you know where the Fourteenth is now?"

The soldier stared down at her and his mouth gaped. "The Fourteenth? *I'm* with the Fourteenth, missy."

"You know my papa? Colonel Birdsong? Is Papa's troop in Indian Territory?"

"Whoa there." The man gave a grandfatherly laugh. "Course I know Colonel Birdsong. But the troop ain't here. I been on furlough, but I can fill you in some." He took off his gray cap while he looked hopefully toward Renny. "You by any chance got some coffee?"

"We've got eggs!" Saranell shouted.

"Eggs?" The soldier wiped his mouth with the back of his hand. "I ain't seen a egg in I don't know how long. They don't have nothing like eggs in the field, nor at home neither."

"Renny, let's have all three eggs," she cried. "Renny's going to cook them on a rock!"

Renny slid her a look that warned her to be quiet, but she wasn't looking at him to see the warning as she held the side of the carriage and watched the man climb down from his horse.

"What happened to your arm, missy?" He let the reins drop, and the black horse padded closer to Toby.

"I broke it. Tell me about the Fourteenth! Tell me about Papa!"

The man brushed his palm over his thin gray hair and gave her a nervous glance. "Now I don't want your egg under no false pretenses, Missy. I ain't sure about the colonel. The troop was aiming for Pittsburgh Landing in Tennessee, but when General Johnston got hisself killed, General Beauregard had to retreat to Mississippi."

Renny dug flint from his pocket, struck sparks onto a bed of dry leaves. He seemed to be paying no attention to the soldier or his conversation.

"That's about when we got a fever outbreak in camp. Them boys from the hills ain't seen diseases, and measles is a real killer, worse than minie balls, so the doctors shunt off the cases of pure sickness when they can. They don't want to mess with measles while they got arms and legs to saw off. So when I come down with them red spots, they let me light out for home."

"And Papa?" Saranell asked.

The man avoided her eyes. "That I can't rightly tell, missy. Last I seen him, he was making for Mississippi with the rest of the troop. That was a couple of weeks ago." He stared down at his cracked leather boots as he replaced the gray cap. "But as far as I know, he's just fine."

Then he fastened his attention on Renny, who was breaking the three eggs onto a flat stone. "My, oh my, don't them eggs smell good." He went over and squatted down beside Renny to watch the yolks bake and the colorless liquid around them solidify white.

As Renny revolved the rock and added more twigs to his fire, the man stood up and went to his saddlebag. When he returned, he carried three squares of hardtack. "It'll be mighty hard to finger up a egg from that hot rock, missy, but we can scoop them on these for easy eating."

He handed the hardtack to Renny, who tended the eggs for another minute before he balanced an egg onto each square and passed one to Saranell, gave the soldier one, and kept the last for himself.

The man's egg was gone in a gulp, but Saranell nibbled the white from the stony bread and savored the yellow, which she had to down in a mouthful. Then she sucked on the square.

When the trooper finished the last of his hardtack, he reached down and gathered the reins of the black horse from the dusty road. "That was a mighty tasty snack. Thankee, little lady."

He swung into his saddle. "Now don't you worry none about your pa. The colonel'll be all right. And you be careful on your journey."

He pressed his heels into the horse's flanks, and the horse ambled past the carriage and up the hill.

Saranell watched them disappear.

"I'd know if Papa was hurt, wouldn't I?" she asked Renny.

"I expect so." He ate his egg and wiped the hardtack dry with his palm.

"I mean I'd feel it, wouldn't I? I'd know if something happened?"

He nodded. "I sense it right away when Captain Thibidoux fall dead in the street." He put the square of bread in his jacket pocket. "When something happen to somebody's papa, they generally know."

20

RENNY KICKED THE EMBERS APART, helped Saranell onto the driver's box, and they set off again under his steady stream of conversation.

Saranell listened, and the sun crossed the middle of the sky to drop toward the horizon while Renny told her about the Fleet Street shop in London where Captain Thibidoux bought red silk pocket handkerchiefs, about the London Tower, where Englishmen—and women—lost their heads on a chopping block for stealing scarlet handkerchiefs.

Saranell glanced over her shoulder, but there was no splash of scarlet in the carriage.

And as if Renny had noticed her glance, he began another story about a freed slave name Frederick Douglass who had been to England and Ireland, where people ate only potatoes.

"Which I wouldn't be minding a bit right now myself," he said.

As twilight softened the landscape, Renny draped the Yankee great coat over her shoulders and talked of fine ladies in New Orleans, who served chocolates decorated with sugared violets and who watched Mardi Gras parades from their iron balconies.

At last he reined Toby to a stop under a patch of oaks.

"We going to have us a good cook fire tonight so we can eat cornpone on sticks," Renny said.

His voice was hoarse as he added, "We need ditchwater to mix with that meal, so you lay back now while I get us fixed up with some good muddy water."

He spread quilts for her on the ground and pulled a sterling bowl from the bag.

He was gone for only a few minutes, and when he came back, he smiled at Saranell through the dusk and started a fire away from the trees.

Saranell watched the sky slowly become a deep blue, then a black, dome. It was so vast and endless that the specks of stars made it the emptiest expanse in the universe. She gazed up at it, and the aloneness of the dark hills merging with the dark sky began to crush her.

Tears ran from the corners of her eyes.

The stars swam and dissolved. And in a moment she was sobbing.

For her mother. For herself. For the awkward balm-of-Gilead trees that were so gray and useless in the winter, and for the smell of books in her father's library.

Renny anchored the bowl on the ground beside the fire and came over to kneel beside her. He put an arm around her shoulders. "I guess it about time for a good cry. I know how it feel to lose people you love. My mama, she sold away when I reach about your same age."

She sobbed, and in a soothing voice he described the last time he'd seen his own mother. "You lucky to know your mama be all right now. You know how she go away and where she at. But some ain't never sure, and that keep the whole thing sore open."

He talked on in his quiet voice, and at last her tears lessened.

She finally wiped her wet face with the back of her hand.

"You doing OK now?"

She nodded.

"I got to build up that fire and put us on them corn balls. You scoot over here and learn some about cooking."

He got up, found a sterling fruit bowl in the sack, and measured a portion of cornmeal into it. He carefully stirred in the ditch water with his fingers. "This part got to be just right. You don't want nothing too thick, nor too runny. It got to hold fast to the stick."

He patted batter onto four stubby branches that he drove into the ground beside the fire.

She wiped her cheeks again and took a jagged breath.

"You keep one side of corn mush toward the heat until it get firm and brown," he instructed. "Then you revolve it so the other side bake good."

She watched him turn the sticks with the bulges of corn batter that resembled wasp nests.

"They smell done."

"Not yet, but they be ready any minute now."

He shook out the blue greatcoat and hung it over her shoulders.

"Ain't nothing tastier than pone roasted the right way by a open fire. But you got to be careful they ain't black on the outside and raw in the middle."

The odors of cornbread and campfire smoke entwined, and Toby neighed.

"We ain't got none for you," Renny said. "You still just a mule and you got to make do with grass."

Saranell's mouth filled with saliva and she clamped her lips and swallowed. "When did we eat last?"

"Maybe a year ago."

He studied the fire, tapped one of the corn pods, and waited. At last he pulled a stick of baked meal from the ground and handed it to her.

She broke off a corner and put the hot crusted dough in her mouth. It burned her tongue and made tears start in her eyes again.

As she blinked them away, she glanced across the fire.

A motionless figure stood under the trees beside Toby.

Saranell gasped and pointed with the stick of cornbread.

Renny looked up as the figure moved slowly toward them.

21

THE MAN CAME out of the darkness, and the firelight showed his Yankee uniform and moccasins. A pair of black braids dangled from beneath his officer's hat.

"Who are you?" he asked in a deep, resonant voice.

"It's an Indian," Saranell whispered.

The man looked at Renny. "Who are you?" he repeated.

"René Thibidoux," Renny said.

The man studied him a long time in the firelight before he nodded. Then he examined Saranell. "And—?"

"Saranell Birdsong," Renny answered for her. "She just a little girl."

"I can see that." He turned back to Renny and pushed the slouch hat away from his forehead. His black hair had been parted sharply down the middle to make the braids. "What are you doing out here?"

"Going to Boggy Depot."

"To meet my Papa," Saranell added quickly.

But the ring of truth and confidence with which she'd first said it in Fort Smith was missing now, and the man gazed silently at her. "I doubt that," he said.

"Well, she hoping her papa be there when we get to the station, and—"

"You're not a runaway since you've got your little mistress along," the man interrupted. "But what in God's name are you doing out here in Indian Territory with a child wrapped in a Union coat?"

"On our way to Texas. She got her aunt there." He didn't explain the coat.

The Indian officer squatted abruptly and studied her face.

Finally he nodded again.

Then he took another stick wrapped with cornmeal from near the fire and handed it to Renny as he stood up.

Renny took it. "I guess you in the Northern army."

The man shrugged. "General Lane supplied us with Union tents and uniforms. But we haven't had to earn them with a battle yet."

He stood rod-straight while he examined their fire, the carriage, the little mule under the trees. "General Lane makes a habit of freeing slaves if you've a mind to hook up with him."

"I got to get the child to Texas."

"I figured as much." He pulled the brim of the hat down on his forehead again. "And on the other side of Texas is Mexico."

Renny looked at him without expression.

The man glanced around their little camp again.

"I passed a patrol of Rebs a couple of days ago. I'd watch out for that mule if I were you."

He moved away without cracking a dry leaf, and his voice floated back in the darkness. "Good luck."

He might have been dark smoke or black mist as he disappeared into the forest.

Toby suddenly whinnied a loud bray.

Renny jumped.

The cornbread in his hand broke apart and tumbled from the stick.

Saranell watched him try to rescue the two halves as they fell toward the fire, and a giggle rose in her throat.

She put her fingers over her quivering mouth to control the laugh as Renny swooped and caught the pieces of cornbread.

But the giggle wouldn't be controlled, and she dropped her hand to laugh.

Renny held the two little canoes of cornbread and looked at her.

Then he threw back his head. His white teeth gleamed in the firelight, and his laughter mingled with hers, became a roar.

Their bodies shook, and their laughter howled into the night until it echoed from the trees and the stars.

22

SARANELL SAT ON THE DRIVER'S BOX with Madison on her lap and stared at the river which spread on both sides of the ferry.

It was a river as wide as a lake.

Another carriage, not as fine as theirs but having a pair of tired horses in the harness, and a wagon, pulled by a team of mismatched mules and loaded with logs, rode the ferry with them. The other landau contained three wounded Confederate soldiers, but only one of them, a man with a missing leg, was conscious. Since the caps of all three were equipped with red crowns rather than the yellow of the Arkansas Fourteenth, Saranell didn't speak to the one-legged man or ask him anything about her father.

She merely watched the approaching Texas shore.

The day before in Boggy Depot Renny had traded another silver tray for a can of peaches. Then he'd bargained away the heavy silver candelabra that once sat on Geneva's dining room table, a candlestick made to hold a dozen candles, for their passage on the ferry at Colbert.

Her father had never liked that particular candle holder anyway, and she hadn't had to watch her tongue while Renny bartered the candlestick away.

They'd met no obstacles, no one seemed surprised by them or stared at them, and since no soldier—not even unwounded ones passing on the road—had shown any interest in them or their little mule, Saranell could sit comfortably on the box while the flatboat neared the far shore.

She examined the water for rose-colored tints, but only the mud on the bank had a color resembling red, and it was more a muted rust than an actual red.

She leaned over and whispered to Renny, who stood beside Toby, "Why do they call this the Red River?"

Before he could answer, one of the wagon mules reared, one of the unconscious soldiers moaned, and Toby stamped his front hooves uneasily.

"Whoa. Easy there."

She didn't ask again, and after a few more minutes and a few more miles of gray river water, the ferry bumped a wooden dock.

The ferryman spat into the water that wasn't red, took down the shabby gate, and kicked blocks from the wheels of the log wagon and the two carriages. He seemed deaf and dumb to everything but the river and its bank.

Renny allowed the other drivers to pull ahead before he led Toby off the ferry planks and onto the pier.

He also let the red-brown dust on the road ahead settle before he climbed onto the box beside Saranell and Madison.

"When are we going to eat the peaches?"

"Few more miles. No use to waste good traveling time to stop and loiter in a picnic."

"I bet we could have traded that tray for two cans."

"Maybe." He grinned at her. "But as I keep mentioning, that silver ain't got much nutrition, and all them merchants with tinned food to trade know we going to stay mighty hungry chewing on them silver trays."

She straightened the sling, propped Madison against it.

"We could punch a hole in the top of the can and sip the juice off the peaches while we're traveling," she suggested hopefully.

"Few more miles."

She sighed.

They rode in silence a while before she said, "Your name's René, isn't it?"

He nodded.

"And that sea captain with the same name was your father, wasn't he?"

He nodded again. He sat silent and held the reins steady for a moment and then he added, "But it don't matter who you call you 'papa' where slavery concerned. Fatherhood don't signify when your mama a slave."

She watched the landscape of yellow bushes with their tints of scratcy green for another mile.

Finally she asked, "What did that Indian soldier mean when he said that Mexico was on the other side of Texas?"

He slid her a look as if he might scowl the way he had in the old days at Balm-of-Gilead.

But then he didn't scowl and said, "Mexico ain't got slaves."

"And you're going there, aren't you?"

He didn't answer but dug in his jacket pocket, took out an object, and put it in her palm. "You mama hand me this to get you to Texas, but I ain't needing payment for doing that."

She looked down at her mother's pearl ring.

It was as if the ring had never existed apart from Geneva's finger, and now Saranell turned its strangeness over in her palm. "I never saw it off Mama's hand," she said.

"That a real nice ring. Something to remember your mama by."

Spots of sunlight gathered in the golden clasps, reflected from the globes of pearl.

"Pearls got a good sheen, ain't they?"

She rocked the ring back and forth in the sun, and the milky bubbles glimmered.

"Mama always said there wasn't anything at the center of a pearl but a sharp grain of sand the oyster had to learn to handle."

He watched her a moment before he said gently, "I guess maybe growing up a little like that oyster making them pearls. Maybe it just learning how to handle them sharp bits as you go along."

She pocketed the ring, stared across the land that was Texas, and resettled Madison in her lap. "Maybe," she said.